THE DAKOTA TRAIL

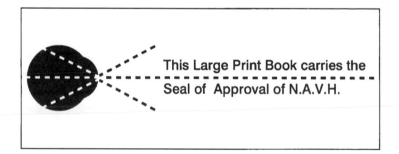

Ralph Compton's

THE DAKOTA TRAIL

ROBERT VAUGHAN

Thorndike Press • Waterville, Maine

This is a work of fiction. Names, characters, places, and incidents either are the product of the author's imagination or are used fictitiously, and any resemblance to actual persons, living or dead, business establishments, events, or locales is entirely coincidental.

Published in 2002 by arrangement with Dutton, a member of Penguin Putnam Inc.

Thorndike Press Large Print Western Series.

The tree indicium is a trademark of Thorndike Press.

The text of this Large Print edition is unabridged.
Other aspects of the book may vary from the original edition.

Set in 16 pt. Plantin by Elena Picard.

Printed in the United States on permanent paper.

Library of Congress Cataloging-in-Publication Data

Vaughan, Robert, 1937–
    Ralph Compton's The Dakota trail : a Ralph Compton
    novel / by Robert Vaughan.
        p. cm.
    ISBN 0-7838-9762-6 (lg. print : hc : alk. paper)
    1. Cattle drives — Fiction.   2. Large type books.
    I. Title: Dakota trail. II. Compton, Ralph. Dakota trail.
    III. Title.
PS3572.A93 D35 2002
    813'.54—dc21   2001051779

The
Dakota
Trail

CHAPTER ONE

Chicago, Illinois

The train that had borne the body of President Abraham Lincoln did not go all the way to Union Station, but stopped instead on a trestle that carried the tracks out over Lake Michigan. When it arrived at eleven o'-clock on the morning of May 1, 1865, it rolled onto the overpass, absolutely silent, save for the mournful tolling of its muffled bell.

The Great Emancipator was, at last, returned to his home state after a twenty-day, cross-country funeral procession in which millions of Americans had turned out to pay their final respects. In city after city, hundreds of thousands of mourners filed by the open coffin for a brief glimpse of their slain martyr. Staring down into the coffin, they saw the slightest suggestion of a placid smile, as well as some discoloration under the right eye from the shock of the bullet wound that had taken his life.

Perhaps three million more had stood alongside the track as the train made its circuitous way from Washington to Illinois. These trackside crowds never diminished, whether it was two o'clock in the afternoon, or two o'clock in the morning. In some cases they waited for hours, often in a pouring rain, with their children beside them. The mothers and fathers sobbed, and the children were shocked and would remember this moment for the rest of their lives. Years later, when they themselves were old men and women, they would write of this event, and pass stories on to their descendants of the time they had watched the grownups weep as the solemn procession rolled by.

As Dick Hodson drove the wagon down Michigan Avenue, he glanced over at the black bunting-draped train and its mirror-image reflected in the lake's still waters. In the engine cab he could see the engineer and fireman, resting now from their labors and engaged in some easy discourse.

A short time earlier, Michigan Avenue had been lined with onlookers, but it was eerily empty now. From the cobblestoned street the clattering hoofbeats of the team and the ringing of the steel-rimmed wheels echoed hollowly, as if the wagon was being drawn through some great hall.

The streets were deserted because the funeral procession was over, and the visitation had begun. Hundreds of thousands of people were downtown at the Cook County Courthouse where, at the rate of seven thousand per hour, they were filing by the catafalque to view Lincoln's body.

Dick didn't see the funeral cortège, nor did he intend to join the throngs who would wait for hours to view the body. Lincoln had been their president, not his. Dick, who had fought for the Confederacy, was a paroled prisoner of war who had been captured at Franklin, Tennessee in one of the last battles of the war.

Captured wasn't quite the word for it. Badly wounded, Sergeant Hodson had been left for dead on the battlefield. A Yankee burial detail, picking up the shattered corpses, noticed that he was still alive. Given only the most rudimentary medical attention, he was taken back to Camp Douglass, Illinois, just outside of Chicago, where more than ten thousand Confederate prisoners of war were kept. Not until he reached the prison camp did a real doctor attend to his wounds. By then he had been left with a permanent limp.

Dick had been paroled just before Lee

surrendered at Appomattox. "Go home, Reb," he was told. "For you, the war's over."

Home, for Dick, was over a thousand miles away in Hutchinson County, Texas. But how was he to get there? He had no money, no food, and a gimpy leg from a war wound.

Then he learned that the Chicago stockyard was hiring men to work their cattle. If there was anything Dick knew, it was cattle, though the idea of being a cowboy in the middle of a city the size of Chicago seemed strange. He took the job, though, informing his employer that he intended to work only long enough to earn enough money to return to Texas.

Dick proved to be a good worker, but it wasn't work that he enjoyed. Being around the cows did not bother him, it was leading them into pens to be slaughtered. He wasn't naïve; he knew the cows his own family had raised on the ranch back in Texas were eventually slaughtered to provide beef. But he had never been part of the killing process, and there was something disturbing about watching a big, muscular man nonchalantly slam a sledgehammer against the head of a cow. Dick avoided the slaughterhouse as much as he could.

By agreeing to work today when everyone else had taken off to go to the funeral procession, Dick was being paid a bonus of ten dollars. That would give him fifty dollars, and achieve the goal he had set for himself. As soon as he delivered this load of salt licks to the warehouse, he intended to quit his job.

Dick drove the wagon into the stockyard, past the holding and feeding pens, beyond the slaughterhouse, all the way back to the warehouse. Backing his wagon into one of the bays, he unhitched and unharnessed the team, turned them into the corral, then began unloading the blocks of salt. Normally there would be one or two people here to help him, but today the stockyard was nearly deserted, and he had to empty the entire wagon by himself.

He was on the last rack when Mr. Clark, his supervisor, arrived. Clark was still wearing the suit he had donned for his sojourn down to the courthouse to view Lincoln's body.

"Almost finished, already? Well, good man, Hodson," Clark said. "Sorry you had to unload all by yourself."

"That's all right. I didn't have anything else to do," Dick said, picking up another block of salt. Clark started to get one as well.

11

"No, don't you do it. You're all dressed up and you'll get yourself mussed. There are only a few more."

Clark smiled and put the block back down. "I guess now that you mention it, my wife would get a little upset if I messed up my Sunday-go-to-meetin' clothes," he said. He took out the makings and began rolling a cigarette as he watched Dick work.

"Did you see Lincoln?" Dick asked as he picked up another salt block and carried it over to the stack.

"Yes. It was a sad thing. All those people crying and all. President Lincoln was a great man."

"From all I've heard, I reckon he was," Dick said. "At any rate, I don't hold with the cowardly way he was killed."

"Yeah, well, the cur who shot him got his comeuppance, all right," Clark said. He handed the cigarette to Dick, lit it for him, then began rolling one for himself.

"Thanks," Dick said, taking a puff.

"Yes, sir," Clark said. He lit his own cigarette before continuing his conversation. "John Wilkes Booth has played his final act. They caught up with the son of a bitch in a barn in Virginia, and shot him down like the dog he was."

Dick off-loaded the final block of salt,

then rubbed his hands together. "That's it," he said.

"I promised you a ten dollar bonus if you would work today, didn't I?" Clark said.

"Yes, sir, I believe you did."

"Well, then, come on into the office and I'll give it to you."

Pinching out and flipping away the butt of his cigarette, Dick followed Clark into the office building where the supervisor opened the safe and took out the money. He counted out ten dollars.

"Hodson, I spoke to the boss about you. I told him you were one of the best workers I have, and I asked him to promote you to foreman of lot three. That's more responsibility, but it'll pay two dollars more per week."

"I appreciate that, Mr. Clark, I really do. But now that I've got enough money to get home, I'll be leaving."

"Leaving? You mean you're quitting?"

"Yes, sir. You remember, I told you a couple of days ago that I would work today but then I would be leaving."

"Yes, I remember, but I figured if you got a promotion you'd be willing to stay. You're a good man, Dick Hodson, even for a Rebel. And, being as you come from the South and were expected to fight for your own people, why, I don't reckon a body could even hold that against you."

"I thank you for that. You've treated me fair, Mr. Clark, and that's the truth. But Chicago is no place for a Texas boy like me. A city makes me feel all closed in. Besides, I haven't seen my folks in over four years."

"Well, I guess I can understand that," Clark said. "All right, Hodson. I won't try and talk you out of it. But how are you going home? The trains don't run all the way to Texas, do they?"

"Not to my part of Texas. I reckon I'll just buy a horse and ride home. The way I figure it, I should be able to cover fifty miles a day. At that rate, I'll be home in three weeks."

"Say, I've got an idea," Clark said. "I read in the paper where the army is selling off some of their remounts at Jefferson Barracks, down in St. Louis. From what the paper said, a fella could get himself a pretty good horse real cheap. If I was you I'd buy a train ticket to St. Louis. That way, you'll not only get a good deal on a horse, you'll be that much closer to Texas."

"Maybe I will do just that," Dick said.

Dick didn't think he had ever seen anything as exciting as the Chicago Railroad Station. A dozen or more tracks converged under the great, vaulting shed, and the air smelled of coal smoke, steam, and teeming humanity. It was a symphony of sound: steel rolling on steel, clanging bells, chugging pistons, rattling cars, shouted orders, and the cacophony of hundreds of individual conversations.

There was a crowd gathered around one of the vendors, a patent medicine man. He was tall and thin, wearing a black suit badly in need of cleaning. His long, bony index finger jabbed at the air as he spoke.

"Yes, ladies and gentlemen, I have come bearing a new miracle drug that will work wonders for the illnesses of all mankind. If you suffer from ulceration of the kidneys, loss of memory, weak nerves, hot hands, flushing in the body, consumption, torpidity of the liver, hot spells, bearing-down feelings, or cancer, this marvelous Extract of Buchu will be your salvation. It will cure the lame and strengthen the weak. And here is something else this medicine will do that no other medicine can do: It will cheer you up when you are blue, and calm you down when you are agitated. It works in all ways of mind, spirit, and body, and this marvelous elixir can be yours for ten cents. Yes, sir, ladies and gentlemen, one-tenth of one dollar, and the miracles of modern medicine can go to work for you right now."

Cure the lame, Dick thought, as he took his seat in the passenger car. If only he could buy some elixir that would make his leg whole again, allow him to walk and run as he could before that Yankee ball shattered bone and destroyed muscle fiber, he would gladly pay any amount.

The train trip from Chicago to St. Louis was an overnight run. Dick had bought the cheapest ticket available, and soon found himself on one of the hard wooden benches of a passenger car known as an "immigrant car." Overcrowded and uncomfortably hot, the car reeked of the smells of strange foods and unwashed bodies.

Dick fell into a fitful sleep. In his dream, it was the last day of November, 1864, and he found himself in the hell that was the battle of Franklin. He saw the body of his commander, General John Adams, who was killed as he attempted a mounted leap over the enemy works. Adams' body lay dead on the ground alongside his dead horse, whose front legs were splintered over the Yankee palisade. They had fought in the darkness, exchanging shot, shell, and cannister on a battlefield that was both illuminated by the constant glare of muzzle flashes and obscured by the thick cloud of gunsmoke. In just a few hours, more were killed than in two days of Shiloh. More died in two hours here than in the entire battles of Stones River and Fredericksburg combined.

And when, at last, the battle was over and the Confederate forces retired from the field, leaving more than half their brigade commanders dead on the ground behind them, Dick Hodson, his leg shattered, was unable to withdraw with them. He lay on the field all night while the Union Artillery, unaware that the Confederates had withdrawn, continued their bombardment.

The cannonade continued, the deep-throated boom of the heavy guns sounding like peals of thunder. From his position on the ground, Dick could follow the huge two-hundred-pound shells by the sputtering red sparks of their fuses as they described a high arc through the sky. The shells screamed loudly during their transit, then slammed down to explode among the dead and dying, the only remaining occupants of the field. Not until the gray morning of the first day of December did the cannons fall quiet, and then only because the Federals finally realized that the Confederates were gone.

The train car passed over a rough section of track and as it jarred and rattled, it shook Dick awake. Opening his eyes, he looked through the window and saw the early morning sun streaming down on the peaceful Illinois countryside. It took him a second to make the transition from the battlefield, and he pinched the bridge of his nose until the last sounds, sights, smells, and terrors of war had passed.

"Look," someone in the car said. "There's St. Louis."

From his side of the car, Dick could see nothing but newly planted farm fields. When he looked through the window on the opposite side of the car, though, he saw the wide Mississippi River and, on the other side of the river, the sprawl of the city of St. Louis.

He felt the train slowing, and the passengers in the car began gathering their belongings, preparing to disembark. Dick didn't move. He had no belongings to gather.

CHAPTER TWO

Although there was talk of building a bridge across the Mississippi River at St. Louis, so far no such structure had been built. As a result, those passengers who were bound for St. Louis and points west had to detrain on the Illinois side of the river, then take the ferry across to the Missouri side.

"Could you tell me where to catch the ferry for Jefferson Barracks?" Dick asked the ferry captain as the passengers began to board.

"You want to go to Jefferson Barracks, sonny, get on board. I'll take you there."

"Thanks."

When the ferry was fully loaded with passengers from the train and a few wagons and local foot passengers, the captain climbed up to the wheelhouse.

"Raise the gangplank!" he called out.

One of the deckhands began cranking a winch, which raised the gangplank.

"Let go bowlines!"

The other deckhand slipped the lines, then the captain pulled on the chain that blew the boat whistle, a deep-throated, two-note harmonious tone audible on both sides of the river. The paddle wheel began spinning backward, and the boat pulled away from the dock. As soon as it was clear, the boat put about, presenting its bow to the western shore. The engine telegraph was slipped to full forward, and the wheel began spinning in the other direction, propelling the boat with surprising speed across the river.

The ferry put in at LaClede's Landing in St. Louis. There was a great exodus at this place, then with only a few passengers remaining, the boat pulled away from the cobblestone bank and went downstream for two miles where it landed at the foot of a series of wooded hills.

"Last stop, boys," the captain called down, and the five remaining passengers — four uniformed soldiers and Dick Hodson — disembarked. Set back in the trees and hills and clearly visible from the river were the red brick and white limestone buildings of Jefferson Barracks, the U.S. Army's biggest and most important military post west of the Mississippi River.

Dick followed a limestone path through

well-tended grounds from the landing up to the fort. As he approached the gate, a sergeant stepped out to meet him.

"You wouldn't be a soldier out of uniform now, would you, mister?" the sergeant challenged.

"No," Dick said.

"Then what's your business here?"

"Is it true that the army has some horses for sale?"

"Aye, lad, 'tis true," the sergeant answered. He pointed. "You'll be findin' the creatures down to the stables. The ones for sale are in lot B."

"I was told I could get a good price," Dick said.

"Aye, the best deal you're going to find, lad. They're captured Secesh horses and you know what good horses them was. A body can have his pick for forty dollars."

"Forty dollars? I was hoping for something a little cheaper."

"Cheaper? Sure, lad, 'n would ye be wantin' the horses for ridin' or for the glue factory?"

"For riding."

"I thought as much. Ridin' is what these horses are for. They are worth a hundred dollars if they are worth ten cents. Go on down and see for yourself."

With a nod of thanks, Dick started toward the stables. He realized that his expectations had been unrealistic, but he had hoped to be able to find a horse for twenty-five to thirty dollars. It didn't have to be a great horse, just one that was healthy and strong enough to get him home.

His first glimpse of the horses validated the sergeant's claim. They were all good animals, well worth the forty dollars that was being asked for them. But as he studied them, he considered the conundrum he faced. If he bought the horse, he would still need a saddle and tack, some beans, flour, salt, coffee, and maybe a little bacon for the trail. He would also need a pistol. But paying forty dollars for a mount wouldn't leave enough money for him to outfit himself for the trail.

With a sigh of frustration, he turned away from the stables when he heard a shout of warning from one of the other lots.

"Cap'n Cavanaugh! Look out, sir! Look out!"

Looking toward the commotion, Dick saw a man on the ground. The horse over him was rampant, and as it came back down, its slashing forelegs barely missed the man's head. Captain Cavanaugh rolled to get away from the horse. The horse reared again, but by now Cavanaugh had positioned himself against a water trough, the only place where he could get away from the flailing stallion.

Without a second thought, Dick grabbed a saddle blanket from the top rail of the fence, then vaulted over and hurried toward the horse, shouting and waving the blanket. Seeing Dick and the flapping blanket, the horse stopped his attack against Cavanaugh and came toward this new irritant.

"Get out of here while I keep him busy!" Dick shouted.

Cavanaugh scrambled toward the fence, where he was helped up and over by eager hands.

Using the blanket as a bullfighter would a cape, Dick managed to entice the horse into one errant pass. The horse corrected himself and reared again, this time launching itself right at Dick. At the last minute, Dick jumped to one side, tossing his blanket at the horse as he did so. The blanket landed on the horse's head, temporarily blinding him. Now the creature reared and whinnied, kicking at the air in rage, as Dick managed to make it back to the fence. The same hands who helped Cavanaugh now reached down to pull Dick over the fence. He just made it when the horse tossed off the blanket. Then, looking around and seeing that his would-be tormentors were gone, the horse shook his head, blew, then trotted back toward the other horses as docilely as if nothing had happened.

"Mister, that was quick thinkin', and I want to thank you," Cavanaugh said.

"It was nothing," Dick said.

"I don't believe Mrs. Cavanaugh would think saving her son was nothing." He stuck out his hand. "The name's Marcus Cavanaugh."

"Yes, I heard one of the men call your name. I'm Dick Hodson."

Captain Cavanaugh looked at Dick's trousers. They were gray, with a narrow, yellow stripe on either side. "A Reb?"

"I was. You have a problem with that?"

Cavanaugh laughed. "Hell no, I don't have a problem with that. You could be a Turkish Moor for all I care. You saved my life, that's all that counts with me."

"I'm glad I could be of some service," Dick said. He turned and started to walk away.

"Hey, wait a minute, where are you going?" Cavanaugh called to him. "The least you could do is let me buy you a drink. No, better than that, why don't you let me buy you dinner?"

Dick hadn't eaten since yesterday, partly because he hadn't taken the time since boarding the train, and partly because he was trying to save money. The idea of a free meal appealed to him, and he stopped and looked back. "All right," he said.

"You saw Lincoln's body?" Captain Cavanaugh asked as he poured himself another beer from the pitcher that sat on the table. The two men were at Lambert's Riverfront Café where they had just enjoyed a meal of fried catfish. The pile of bones in front of them gave mute testimony to the number of fiddlers they had dispatched.

"No, I didn't go to see the body," Dick answered. "But I did see the train. It was quite impressive looking."

"The country is going to miss President Lincoln. And you want to know what I think? I believe the South is going to miss him more than the North."

"Why would you say that?"

"There's a strong difference of opinion as to how to treat the South, now. Lincoln wanted to take the prodigal son approach, you know, welcome the rebellious states back with open arms. Others in the government feel that some retribution is in order. And now, with Lincoln dead, I'm afraid those people have come to the ascendancy. They will more than likely get what they want."

"You may be right about that," Dick agreed, as he poured himself another beer.

"So, you didn't like the looks of any of the horses the army had to sell?" Cavanaugh asked.

"That's not it. I thought there were some great-looking horses there. I was just hoping to find something a little cheaper."

"Cheaper than forty dollars? Forty dollars is a damn good price when you consider what you are getting."

"I agree. But if I spend forty dollars for a horse, I won't have enough money left to go back to Texas."

"I see what you mean. So, what are you going to do now?"

"Get a job and earn a little more money, I guess. It's been this long, what's another month?"

"Work? Wait a minute, are you looking for a job?"

"Yes. Why, do you know of one?"

"I know a job that would be perfect for you. The pay is one hundred dollars, and it won't take you more than a week. And if you are any good at it, you could wind up with a free horse when the job is over."

"Wait a minute. The job only lasts a week, and I'll make one hundred dollars *and* get a free horse?"

"Whether or not you get the horse depends on how well you do the job," Cavanaugh replied.

Dick shook his head. "I don't know. This sounds too good to be true. Is it legitimate? Who do I have to shoot?"

"You don't have to shoot anyone, and I assure you, it is legitimate. The job is horse-wrangler. I'm taking a platoon of cavalrymen and thirty horses to Omaha City. My second-in-command is a brand-new second lieutenant, and all the cavalrymen are green troops, so I'm going to need someone to look after the horses, at least until we get there."

"Omaha City? Where's that? I've never heard of it."

"It's in Nebraska, just across the Missouri River from Council Bluffs, Iowa. We'll be going up by riverboat. What do you say, Mr. Hodson, would you like the job? Lieutenant Kirby and I could really use you."

"That would be north of here, wouldn't it?"

"And west. So, while you are going farther north, away from your home, you make up for it by going west, closer to where you live."

Dick took another swallow of his beer as he contemplated the offer. "That's true, isn't it?" he pondered aloud. "All right, Captain Cavanaugh, you've got yourself a horse-wrangler."

"Good!" Cavanaugh said. "We leave tomorrow."

For the first ten miles of their journey they were traveling up the Mississippi, beating their way against the strong, six-mile-per-hour current. As they negotiated a wide, sweeping bend, the steam relief pipe boomed as loudly as if the city of St. Louis were under attack by a battery of cannons. Finally they turned into the mouth of the Missouri, and the real trip was begun.

For the rest of the day the riverboat *Western Commerce* worked its way up the Missouri River, its two engines clattering, the paddle wheel slapping at the water, and the boat enveloped in a thick smoke that belched forth from the high twin chimneys.

By nightfall of the first day they were near the town of Washington, Missouri. As the crow flies, Washington was a distance of no more than forty-five miles from St. Louis, though they had already navigated ninety miles through the twisting river.

Dick went forward to check on the horses.

Captain Cavanaugh had told him he was bringing thirty mounts, but in fact there were thirty-two horses. He counted them twice to make certain he was right.

"All the army actually needs is thirty horses," Lieutenant Kirby said. The young lieutenant had been standing at the bow, watching the river roll by when Dick came up to make his count. "So we only have thirty on the manifest. The extra two horses are to replace any that we may lose along the way."

"What if all thirty-two of them make it?" Dick asked.

Captain Cavanaugh, who had also seen Dick count the horses, now came forward to answer Dick's question.

"If we have more than thirty when we get there, I am authorized to dispose of the excess by whatever means I may choose. And what I will choose is to give them to you. But of course that is only if there are any left over. Therefore, it will behoove you to get them all there alive."

"I'll get them all there, even if I have to sleep with them," Dick promised.

Every horse did make it and, true to his word, Captain Cavanaugh gave Dick the two extra mounts. Dick thought about trying to take both of them back to Texas with him but finally decided to sell one. He got one hundred dollars from the sale, plus another hundred dollars in payment for his services as a wrangler. Even after buying saddle and tack, a new outfit, pistol and holster, and a long gun, he still had close to two hundred dollars left.

Figuring that he owed Cavanaugh a drink, he arranged for Captain Cavanaugh and Lieutenant Kirby to meet him at the Bull's Head Saloon. He was on his second drink when Cavanaugh came in.

"Where's Lieutenant Kirby?" Dick asked.

"He's got duty officer," Cavanaugh replied. He nodded toward the front of the saloon. "I saw your horse tied up out there. When are you leaving?"

"Today. Right after we eat."

"I wish you good luck."

"So far, you've been my good luck," Dick said. "I got the job and the horses, thanks to you. I guess I'm glad I didn't kill you at Chancellorsville," he joked. Though they hadn't actually seen each other at Chancellorsville, they discovered during the long conversations they had on the trip upriver that both had fought in that battle. Dick laughed. "Never thought I'd find a Yankee I could call a friend," he said. "But you and Kirby have been very nice to me."

"Well, I can't speak for Kirby, mind you, but I'm not your run-of-the-mill Yankee," Cavanaugh teased. "I'm Marcus Cavanaugh of the Back Bay Cavanaughs. My people are fine people, or so my grandmother likes to remind me. What about your people?"

Dick laughed. "Haven't you heard? The entire state of Texas is populated by brigands and horse thieves who have been run out of other states. I've no doubt but that my ancestors fit right into that category." He stood, then extended his hand. "At any rate, it has been a pleasure knowing you, Captain." He turned then, and started toward the door.

"Mr. Hodson, how would you like to meet again in about five months?" Cavanaugh called to him.

Dick stopped in his tracks. He knew his new Yankee friend well enough now to realize that this wasn't a casual inquiry. He turned back and studied Cavanaugh through narrowed eyes. "What are you talking about?"

"Next week I'll be taking my platoon out to Fort Sully. That's up in the Dakota Territory. Now that the war is over, quite a few men are being transferred into the Northwest Territories to keep the Indians pacified. It's going to take a lot of beef to feed that many men. If you could get your cattle up there before winter sets in, the army will pay you forty dollars a head. Seems to me like an enterprising young man like you might be able to put out several hundred head or so."

"How many head do you think the army would take? Would they take more than a thousand?"

Cavanaugh laughed. "More than a thousand head? My, you are ambitious, aren't you?"

"I'm just thinking ahead, is all."

Cavanaugh nodded. "Yes, Mr. Hodson. The army will take more than a thousand head."

With a broad smile on his face, Dick returned to the table and once again stuck out his hand. "Well then, this isn't goodbye. This is 'I'll see you later.' "

"Oh, I think there's one thing you should know," Cavanaugh said.

"What's that?"

"Don't waste a whole lot of time getting your herd together. Not only will you need to get started right away to get your herd up there before the first snow, you've also got another worry. I told you there are some people who are wanting retribution. From what I hear, Congress is planning to pass laws that will greatly restrict your right to move around, let alone move an entire herd out of the state."

"Why would they do something like that?"

"They want to punish the South for killing Lincoln."

"Hell, Captain, the South didn't have anything to do with killing Lincoln. That was John Wilkes Booth."

"Doesn't matter. Lincoln's dead and people want revenge. My advice to you is to get your herd out of Texas as fast as you can."

Dick nodded at Cavanaugh. "Good advice," he said. "I think I'll heed it."

CHAPTER THREE

Hutchinson County, Texas

Dick Hodson was tired. It wasn't just the tiredness of the long ride back to Texas from Omaha City. Added to it was a bone-deep, butt-tired exhaustion from four years of war and four months of prison. As he rode south along the Brazos, he put a little more weight in the stirrups and switched positions to get some relief from the saddle weariness.

Just ahead he saw a building. It was obvious that at one time it had been an inn, but over the years it had been enlarged to accommodate a store, a barbershop, and even a couple of rooms out back for sleeping. A crudely lettered sign nailed to one of the porch supports read: FOOD, DRINK, GOODS. BEDS TEN CENTS, BLANKETS FIVE CENTS.

The result of all the additions was a rambling, unpainted wooden structure that stretched and leaned and bulged and sagged until it looked as if the slightest puff of wind might blow it down.

It had been over a week since Dick had eaten anything other than his own trail cooking, or drunk anything besides water or coffee. The prospect of a hot meal and a cold beer was appealing to him, so he sloped his horse down a shallow hill, then dismounted in front of the establishment.

There were two men in blue uniforms sitting on a bench out front. One was a big man with a bushy red beard. The sergeant's stripes he was wearing were the light blue color of infantry, though his tunic was so dirty that the chevrons barely showed. The other man was beardless and his sleeve was bare, except for the ghost-shadow of where stripes had once been. He was rail-thin and hard-looking. The two Union soldiers studied Dick as he dismounted.

What they saw was an average-sized man of twenty-one, who looked thirty. Dick was wearing denim trousers and a gray, broadcloth shirt. There was nothing in his dress to indicate that he had ever been a soldier, but when one looked beyond his dress, into his face, one could read his entire history. Like hundreds of thousands of other men in gray, Dick was a forgotten soldier in the defeated army that had served the failed cause of a now-defunct nation.

The big Yankee scratched his beard while the other spat a stream of tobacco juice onto the dirt. They studied Dick, but neither of them spoke. Dick nodded wordlessly at them as he stepped up onto the porch.

A nondescript yellow dog was sleeping in the shade provided by the porch roof, so secure with his position and the surroundings that he didn't even open his eyes as Dick stepped around him to go inside.

The interior of the inn was a study of shadow and light. Some of the light spilled through the door, and some peeked through windows which were nearly opaque with dirt. Most of it, however, was in the form of shafts of sunbeams that stabbed through the gaps between the boards. These bars of light were filled with gleaming dust motes that hung suspended in the still air.

Dick heard a scratching noise coming from the back of the room and when he looked toward the sound he saw a young woman on her hands and knees, using a pail of water and a stiff brush to scrub the floor. She glanced up at Dick and brushed a strand of pale brown hair back from her forehead. Her eyes were gray and one of them tended to cross. When she smiled, she displayed the gap of a missing tooth.

"Mister, you lookin' for someone to warm your bed?" the woman asked, hopefully.

"No, thanks," Dick answered.

Showing her disappointment, the woman went back to her scrubbing. The proprietor came out of one of the back rooms then, wiping his hands on the apron that, at one time, might have been white.

"What can I do you for?"

"Thought maybe I'd get a cold beer and somethin' hot to eat," Dick said.

"Got no beer. Got some whiskey, though. And steak, taters, and biscuits to eat. The biscuits is particular good. My girl, Mary Lou, made 'em." He nodded toward the woman on her hands and knees.

"That'll do fine," Dick said. He took a table over in the corner of the room.

"Take the man his whiskey, Mary Lou," the proprietor ordered.

Mary Lou got up from the floor and took the glass of whiskey to Dick. She leaned over the table as she set the glass in front of him, affording him an eyeful of her ample breasts. She smiled another silent invitation, and Dick actually felt some sympathy for her. During the war, when any warm female body would be welcome company to a lonely soldier, Mary Lou probably did all right. But the dissipation of her profession,

37

plus the missing tooth and misshapen nose which Dick suspected were the results of a few violent encounters with drunken soldiers, had given her a face that would be hard-pressed to attract customers during normal times.

Dick smiled back at her, but did nothing to encourage any further solicitation.

"Here you go," the proprietor said a few minutes later, putting the food on the table in front of him. "Don't mean to be buttin' in, but, even though you ain't in uniform, looks to me like you was in the war."

"I was."

The proprietor smiled, and hit his fist into his hand. "I know'd it," he said. "And you was one of our'n I bet."

"I was with the Fourth Texas Cavalry."

"I had me a boy in Hancock's Texas Brigade." The proprietor nodded toward Mary Lou, who was once more scrubbing the floor. "He's her brother. We ain't heard nothin' from him for near 'bout a year now. His name is Tanner. Jimmy Tanner. You by any chance run across him?"

"Sorry, I haven't," Dick replied as he carved off a bite of steak. As he looked at the pink, bleeding piece of meat and sniffed the aroma, he actually began to salivate. It had been over four years since he had tasted steak.

"Tell the truth, I'm beginning to get some- what worried about 'im," the proprietor said.

"I wouldn't worry yet. There are thousands, probably tens of thousands of men still out on the roads, making their way back home. If he was a long way off and afoot, it'll take him a while."

"Yes, sir, that's what we keep a'tellin' ourselves. You likin' the steak?"

"It's delicious."

"You can have another one at no extra charge if you want it. Here in Texas, beef is so cheap right now, you can't give a steer away."

Dick looked up in surprise. "That's not good to hear," he said. "My folks have a cattle ranch up in Hutchinson County, near Windom."*

"Then they're prob'ly havin' as much trouble as ever'one else. Cows ain't worth what it costs to feed em."

"Why is that?"

"I reckon it's 'cause so many boys went off to fight in the war that there wasn't nobody left at home to take the cattle to market. Now there's so many cows they're near 'bout

---

*Windom no longer exists, but it is near the present-day location of Stinnett.

overgrazing. I've heard tell that some folks has even started killing off their cattle."

"Yes, but now that the war's over, the market will come back," Dick said.

"Hey, you!" a gruff voice called. "You a Rebel soldier?"

Looking toward the sound of the voice, Dick saw that the big, red-bearded Yankee sergeant and his skinny friend had stepped inside.

"I was. Something I can do for you, gents?"

"See there, Poke, he answered to Reb," the sergeant said. "I told you he was one."

"Yeah, you had 'im figured, all right," the skinny soldier replied. He squirted a stream of tobacco juice in the general direction of a spittoon but missed. It made a new stain on the already mottled floor.

"Mister, you ain't showin' your colors. You ain't wearin' no Reb uniform. Why is that?"

"The war's over and I'm going home," Dick said without elaboration.

"Well, you see now, here's the thing, Reb. Me 'n Poke was takin' us a look at that horse you're ridin'. And what do you know, but that it's wearin' a U.S. brand."

"I believe it is," Dick said.

"You admit it's a U.S. brand?"

"How can I deny it? It's there, plain to see."

"How'd you come by it?"

"How I came by it isn't important. It's my horse."

"That's all you're goin' to say? That it's your horse?"

"That's right."

"Well, that ain't a good enough answer, mister. Now, me and Poke here, we're a'needin' us a horse. And seein' as how the one you're ridin' is U.S. Government issue, I think we'll just take yours."

"Oh, I wouldn't advise that."

The sergeant laughed. "He wouldn't advise it," he said to Poke. Poke laughed with him.

"But if you think you can take him, go ahead."

"What do you mean, if I think we can take him? There's two of us. There's only one of you."

Dick stared coldly at the Yankee sergeant and his skinny friend. "There may be only one of me, but I have two bullets," Dick said, calmly.

The sergeant laughed again. "So, all you have to do is pull your gun and start shooting. Is that it?"

"No," Dick answered. While he was

41

talking, Dick, his action concealed by the table, had eased his pistol from his holster. Now he brought his hand up and cocked the pistol. It made a deadly-sounding click as the sear engaged the cylinder. "All I have to do is start shooting. I've already pulled my gun."

The bearded sergeant realized he had just been tricked. Dick now had the drop on him.

"No, now, just wait a minute there, mister," the Yankee said, holding his hands out as if to stop Dick. "We ain't got nothin' in mind like that. We was just curious, that's all."

"Shuck your pistols, lay them on the floor, then go sit at the table over there. Mr. Innkeeper, I want you to give both of these boys a whiskey on me."

"Yes, sir," the innkeeper replied.

Dick watched the Yankees pull their guns out of their holsters and lay them on the floor. He made a motion with his pistol and they moved over to the table he had pointed out. The innkeeper brought them each a drink.

"The war's over, boys," Dick said. "We can keep on killing each other, or we can start trying to live together. Which will it be?"

"We got nothin' ag'in you personal, Reb," the sergeant said.

Dick put his pistol on the table in front of him, then lifted his glass toward them. "Then I'd say we've made a good beginning," he replied, toasting them.

The next day, Dick rode down the main street in Windom, Texas. As he looked around at the town, he realized that it was no longer the town of his youth. There was an empty lot where the school once stood. Dunnigan's General Store was now Bloom's Mercantile. The feed store, apothecary, and hardware stores also had new names, names he had never heard before.

The streets were crowded with soldiers in blue uniforms. Yankees crowded the saloons and filled the streets with their loud talk and frequent laughter.

There were also some men in tattered gray, defeat and despair evident in their faces. He recognized a few of them. He saw Freddie Lewis sitting in the sun, an empty trouser leg where his right limb should be. Freddie and Dick had once been a team, of sorts. Freddie was one of the fastest runners in the state. Dick was one of the best rifle shots, and the two often performed at the various town and county fairs. They not only won the prize money, but often wound up taking home additional winnings from wagers they had placed on each other.

Dick and Freddie made eye contact. Although the two men had been friends in happier days, now neither had it in him to speak. Instead, Dick nodded, Freddie nodded back, and Dick rode on.

He finally stopped at the gate which led to the Hodson family ranch. The sign read:

TRAILBACK RANCH

JOHN HODSON, PROPRIETOR

EST. 1841

A grasshopper was clinging to the faded lettering and a clump of weeds had grown up around the sign. Dick dismounted and pulled the weeds so that the sign was clearly visible.

"This sign needs to be redone," Dick said to the horse. Talking to his horse was a habit he had gotten into during the long ride back. He knew it was a barely disguised way of talking to himself, but often on the long, lonely trail, he felt the need speak aloud, if only to keep himself sane.

Tossing the weeds he had pulled aside, he remounted. The saddle creaked under his weight and he looked up and down the fence row. He had never seen the place looking so unkempt, and he wondered how his father had let it get so run down.

The house was half a mile from the gate, and he found himself quickening the pace until, finally, he urged the horse into a gallop for the last quarter mile.

"Mom! Dad!" he shouted as he rode into the front yard and swung down from the saddle. "I'm home!"

At that moment the front door to the house opened, and John and Delia Hodson came outside. As soon as Delia saw her son, her face broke into a broad smile.

"Dick!" she shouted, holding her arms wide. She beat his father to him, and Dick embraced her warmly. He caught a scent of flour and cinnamon as he held her to him, and it was as if he had told her goodbye only yesterday, rather than four and a half years ago.

John stood back as mother and son embraced, then finally Dick released his mother and reached for his father. "Dad!" he said, taking his father in an embrace as well.

The instant he did so, he realized something was wrong. His father had always been a strong man, yet now he seemed frail.

Pulling away from him, he looked into his father's face and saw confusion.

"Dick," John said. His voice was as weak as his embrace had been. "It is good that you're home."

Dick looked at his mother with the unspoken question in his eyes.

"He's been this way for the better part of a year," Delia said. "Ever since the apoplexy."

"He had a seizure?"

Delia nodded, as tears filled her eyes.

"I had a seizure, I didn't die," John said. "You don't need to talk about me as if I'm not here." For that moment, at least, his voice was strong and firm enough to remind Dick of the father he remembered. Dick laughed.

"I can see you're still here," he said. "And cantankerous as always."

"You picked a good time to come home, boy," John said, turning toward the house. "Your mother just baked an apple pie."

CHAPTER FOUR

Dick was finishing his second piece of pie, topped with melted cheese. He had been answering a steady stream of questions ever since he got home.

"We got a letter from you not long after you was captured," Delia said. "And then another one saying that you was turned loose and would be home soon as you made enough money for the fare. So we wasn't worried none about whether you was dead or alive. But I wrote to you several times in between and never heard nothin' back."

"I'm sorry, Mom, I only got one letter from you, and I answered it," Dick said. "And I wrote you several times, besides, but the Yankees wouldn't always deliver them for us."

"Well, it's all behind us now," Delia said. "We can pick up the pieces of our life and go on. There's lots of folks in the county can't even do that. So many of our young men were killed in this war. And for what?"

"What would you have done, Delia? Just let the Yankees have their way?" John asked. "We had no choice but to fight."

"All right, so we fought. And we got our young men killed, and in the end, the Yankees *are* having their way. So what did it all accomplish?"

"Let's don't discuss the war anymore," Dick said with a dismissive wave of his hand. "I've had enough of it."

"Of course you have," Delia. "And I agree."

"Dad, how many head of cattle do we have?"

"I'm not sure," John answered. "I haven't done a roundup in a couple of years. What with everyone gone, it's been difficult to hire hands. And I couldn't do it by myself."

"Though Lord knows he tried," Delia put in, reaching over to pat her husband's hand.

"Do we have five hundred head?"

"Five hundred? Oh, yes, I expect so. Considerable more than that, I would say."

"Great!"

John shook his head. "Not that it's going to do us any good," he said. "Right now the cost of beef is so low it's not worth taking a cow to market. Why, I've even heard that there are thousands of head running wild, like the buffalo used to."

"What if I told you I knew where I could get forty dollars a head?"

John had been slumping, but at hearing that, he sat up straight. "Forty dollars a head? Who would be crazy enough to pay forty dollars a head?"

"The U.S. Army."

"You would sell beef to the same people you fought for nearly five years?" John asked.

"The war's over. If the army is willing to pay forty dollars a head for our beef, then I'm willing to sell it to them."

"If the army is paying forty dollars a head, why isn't everyone selling to them?" Delia asked.

"Because they will only pay that in the Dakota Territory. We've got to take the beef to them."

"The Dakota Territory? That's a long way from here, isn't it?" Delia asked.

"Yes, ma'am, it is. It's about as far as you can go before running into Canada."

John shook his head. "Well, there you go then. You may as well say that they are buying cattle on the moon, for all the good it will do us."

"It will do us plenty of good," Dick said. "I'm taking a herd up."

John snorted and shook his head no.

"Son, I'm afraid that Yankee prison camp made you a little daft. I've had a seizure and I don't always think straight, but even I know there's no way you can get a herd from here to someplace up in the Dakota Territory."

"Sure I can, Dad," Dick said. "I asked how many cows they would take, and they said as many as I can get up there. So, I figure I'll get Charley Konda, Muley Sietz, Mickey Winters, and Billy Votaw to ride with me. I'll let them put in five hundred head also. Maybe a couple of the other boys if they are back. We can put together a herd and an outfit and push the cattle up there before winter sets in."

John began shaking his head slowly, and tears started down Delia's cheeks.

"What is it? You don't think they would like to make a little money from their cattle?"

"Honey, all those boys you mentioned? Charley, Muley, Mickey and Billy? They're all dead. Killed in the war."

Dick let out a small gasp of surprise. "My God," he said. "All of them?"

"Every last one of them. The Blackburn brothers too. And Perry Driscoll."

Dick was quiet for a long moment. "Is there no one left?"

"Just the ones who were either too young or too old to go," John said. "So you can see what I mean when I said I couldn't hire enough hands to do a roundup."

Dick got up from the table and walked over to stare through the window. Charley Konda had been his best friend, and he saw the tree from which Charley had fallen back when they were boys, breaking his arm. Muley's initials were carved in that tree. That tree was also where Dick, Charley, and Muley hid Mickey Winters' clothes when he went skinny-dipping down in the creek. Mickey had to stay in the water all day, then sneak home through the dark that night.

He felt a lump come to his throat and tears sting his eyes.

"I'm sorry, Dick. I thought you knew," Delia said, realizing that her son was hurting.

"No," Dick said. His voice nearly broke and he had to clear his throat before he could speak again. "I hadn't heard. I guess I always expected one or two might not come back. But never in my worst nightmare did I think all of them would be killed."

"You can see what I mean, then, when I say that it is impossible to get the cattle up to where you would have to go."

Dick shook his head, then turned to face

his mother and dad. His face was even more resolute than before. "Difficult, perhaps," he said. "But not impossible. I'm going to do it."

"How?"

"I haven't figured that out yet. But I am going to do it."

"Dick, please, no," Delia said. "I just got you back. Lord in heaven, I don't know what I would do if anything happened to you now."

"Nothing's going to happen, Mom, except that I'm going to get those cows to the Dakota Territory."

The Tilting K Ranch

The next morning's sun, just beginning to gather heat and brilliance, rose in the east above the gently rolling hills. A dark gray haze was still hanging in the notches, though it was already beginning to dissipate, burning off like drifting smoke.

Onto this scene rode Marline Konda, a boyishly slim but gently rounded young woman of twenty. She was quite athletic, but strawberry-blond hair and golden eyes saved her from having a tomboyish appearance. She picked her way carefully along a trail that lead to a private place, a secret glen she had discovered as a little girl, and to which she often came when troubled or when she wanted to be alone.

The trail climbed up the backside of a bluff through a cathedral arch of cedar trees, across a level bench of grass, then out onto a rocky precipice. It was the precipice that made the ride worthwhile, for from it Marline could see the entire ranch, including the main house and the bunkhouses where, before the war, the men who worked here slept when they weren't out on the range or in one of the line shacks. Once, her father's ranch, the Tilting K, had employed as many as forty riders. Now only two men, Pete Malone and George Tolliver, worked on the place and they were too old to do any real work. They did little more than odd jobs, for which they were paid in found.

Marline knew that even if there were enough young men available to run the ranch, her father couldn't afford to pay them now. What had once been a productive ranch was now little more than a subsistence farm. And it would stay that way unless — or until — the price of cattle became high enough to make it profitable to round up the stock and sell.

Below her, a wispy pall of woodsmoke lay

over the house, and Marline knew that her mother was cooking breakfast. Her father would just be waking now, and he would find her note, telling him she had gone for an early ride. It wasn't an unusual practice so he wouldn't be alarmed, nor would he be angry with her for missing breakfast.

Marline sat on the ledge watching as Pete and George made their way from the bunkhouse to the main house for their breakfast. There was a time when the cookhouse was used and at breakfast time it would be filled with laughing cowboys as they prepared for their day's work. Now the cookhouse was boarded shut and the only two hands ate in the main house with the family. Most of the time Marline ate with them, but today she remained here, on the precipice, until Pete and George left the house and walked out to the barn to begin their chores. A short time later she saw her mother come out onto the back porch and toss out the pan of water she had used for washing the breakfast dishes. Finally, she got up, walked back to her horse, mounted, and rode back down to the house.

"Did you have a nice ride?" Marline's mother asked when she came back to the house.

"Yes, thank you."

"There's some coffee on. And I saved you a couple of biscuits. After you've had your breakfast, you'll help me with the laundry? I have to make some soap."

"Yes, Mama, I'll just have some coffee, then I'll be there," Marline said.

When Marline poured herself a cup of coffee, she saw her father sitting at the kitchen table, working over some numbers. "Good morning, Papa," she said. Bringing the pot over to him, she freshened his cup for him. "What are you figuring?"

Joel Konda sighed, then leaned back in the chair and looked across the table at his daughter. "You may as well know," he said. "I'm going to sell the ranch."

"What?" Marline gasped. "Dad, you can't be serious!"

"I've been offered a good price for it," Joel said.

"What's a good price?"

"Well, admittedly it's less than one-third of what it was worth before the war. But let's face it, Marline. If we don't sell it this year, we'll lose it next year in taxes. We aren't making ends meet."

"Grandpa started the Tilting K," Marline said. "He passed it down to you and you were going to . . ." She stopped in mid-sentence.

"Pass it down to Charley? You're right, I was. But Charley isn't here anymore." He pointed outside. "His grave marker is out there on that hill, but his body isn't. He's buried up in Missouri, somewhere, either in an unmarked grave, or under one of those crosses that says 'Unknown.'"

Marline stepped behind her father's chair and draped her arms around his neck. The lack of a body to bury had hurt Joel Konda almost as much as the loss of his son had. For two years he had dwelled upon the fact that they didn't know where he was and couldn't bring him back to lie in the family plot on the ranch.

"Papa, if you sell the ranch, where will we go? How will we live?"

Joel snorted what might have been a laugh. "We'll live a lot better than we are living now, that's for sure," he said. He reached up to take Marline's hand in his. "Look, darlin', I know this place is special to you. I even know about your secret hideout."

"You do?" Marline asked, surprised at the revelation.

"I've known about it since you were twelve. Actually, I've known about it a lot longer than that. It was my hideout when I was young. I have to say I was a little surprised when you found it before Charley."

"Charley knew about it, but he let me keep it for my own."

"The point I'm making, Marline, is that you'll more than likely be getting married someday and when you do, you'll leave the ranch anyway. So it shouldn't be that big of a thing for you."

"And just who would you suggest that I marry, Papa? Most of the boys in the county were killed in the war. The only ones who weren't were either too young to go or too cowardly. I don't want anything to do with any of them. If we could just sell the cattle, we'd be all right. I know we would."

"Yes, if we could just sell the cattle," Joel said. "But that's not likely to happen. The only way we are going to get out of this fix is to sell the ranch."

"Who has made the offer?"

"You know who."

"Not Bryan Phelps?"

"Yes."

"Papa, if you have to sell it, don't sell it to him. I don't trust him. There is something evil about that man."

"That may be so, but he is the only one who has any money now. He's trying to buy every ranch in the valley. The people who sell to him at least get something for their ranch. The ones who try to hold on wind up losing their ranch, and Phelps gets it just by paying the back taxes. In fact, about the only ranch he hasn't tried to buy is Trailback."

"Why hasn't he tried to buy Trailback? You've said many times that Trailback was the finest ranch in the county."

"It is. It's the plum of the valley. The headwater of half a dozen springs and creeks are on that ranch. Phelps knows that John Hodson can hang on the longest, but he also knows that if he can get control of all the ranches that surround Trailback, Hodson will be left fighting the battle all alone."

"And you are going to help Phelps by selling our ranch to him?" Marline asked.

"Honey, we are in a worse fix than John Hodson. Our main source of water is McCamey Creek. It passes through three ranches before it reaches us. If Phelps gets control of any one of those ranches, he can shut us off from water. It's just a matter of time. We either sell to him now, or let him buy it for taxes next year."

"Pa, there has to be another way. There has to be something we can do."

Joel shook his head sadly. "Honey, if you'll just tell me what that something might be, I'll be more than glad to do it," he said. "But right now, I see nothing for us but to sell the land."

When Joel returned to his figuring, Marline knew that he was closing off the conversation. Turning away, she walked out onto the back porch to help her mother.

An unpleasant odor came from a bubbling cauldron that hung over a fire in the back yard. Marline's mother, Trudy, was making soap from lye and the lard rendered from the last hog butchering. The lye came from ashes saved from the fireplace. The ashes had been thrown into a barrel between layers of straw, then water was added, and what dripped out through a seephole in the bottom of the barrel was lye. Trudy was stirring the boiling lard, and she nodded at her daughter, indicating that Marline should fill a dipper with lye and pour it in.

"Mama, Papa can't sell the ranch," Marline said. "He mustn't."

"Honey, do you think for one minute that your father wants to sell this place? This is his entire life. But if we are going to lose it anyway, then he is right to sell it while we can still get something for it."

"We aren't going to lose it," Marline said as she poured in the lye. "I won't let us lose it."

"Don't torture yourself so, daughter," Trudy said. "How are you going to keep us from losing the ranch?"

"I don't know yet. But I swear to you and to Papa, we will not lose this ranch."

Chapter Five

When Dick rode into town, he saw that there was a fistfight in progress in the street in front of the saloon. One of the combatants was a Yankee soldier, in uniform. The other was a civilian. The civilian was younger, but he was as big as the soldier, and he was more than holding his own.

Dick would've gone on into the saloon and left the two men to their fight until he got a closer glimpse of the young civilian. "Muley Sietz!" he gasped.

But that couldn't be, Muley was dead. Then he realized with a start that it wasn't Muley, it was his younger brother, Ron Sietz. Ron wasn't much more than thirteen or fourteen when Dick had left, which would make Ron eighteen today.

Ron was obviously still a kid, but he was strong and whatever it was that started the fight had filled him with resolve. At first there had been a sly smirk on the soldier's face. He would play with the boy for a moment or two, then teach him a lesson.

But the boy was proving to be a difficult student.

The soldier swung hard with a roundhouse right, and Ron countered with a left jab to the soldier's nose. It was considerably more than a light jab, because Dick saw the soldier's nose go flat, then almost immediately begin to swell. The soldier let out a bellow of pain, and a trickle of blood started down across his moustache.

"You Secesh son of a bitch!" the soldier shouted. "I'm going to knock your block off!" He swung with another roundhouse right, missing it as well, and this time Ron caught him with a right hook to the chin. The blow rocked the soldier back but didn't knock him down.

By now, quite a crowd had gathered to watch the fight and everyone was rooting for their champion. To Dick's surprise, there seemed to be about as many soldiers cheering Ron on as there were supporting the soldier.

Ron scored with two more sharp jabs, and it became obvious that the soldier was on his last legs. He was stumbling about, barely able to stay on his feet. Ron set him up for the finishing blow when another soldier suddenly grabbed him from behind. With his arms pinned, he was an easy target for a quick roundhouse right thrown by the first soldier.

Ron's knees buckled, but he didn't go down. Before his adversary could throw another punch, though, Dick brought the butt of his pistol down on the head of the man who had grabbed Ron. The interloper collapsed like a sack of potatoes and, though Dick was prepared to have to defend his action if need be, he found himself cheered by the crowd, civilian and soldier alike.

With his arms free, Ron was able to finish the fight in two more blows, setting his man up with a hard left jab, then dropping him with a vicious right cross.

With the fight over and nothing to hold the spectators' interest, the crowd broke up. Several soldiers dragged their beaten comrade away with them. Within a minute, Ron was standing in the middle of the street, all alone, breathing hard from the exertion.

It wasn't until that moment that Dick realized the fight hadn't been as one-sided as he had thought. Ron had a split lip and a swollen eye. The boy walked over to the watering trough and dipped his handkerchief into the water.

"Here, let me do that," Dick said, taking

Ron's handkerchief and dabbing lightly at his lip.

"Thanks, Dick," Ron said.

"What was the fight about?"

"He called Cassie Thomas a whore."

"Who is Cassie Thomas?"

"She's a whore," Ron said easily.

Dick laughed. "Then I don't understand. If she is a whore, why the fight?"

"Because she's one of our own. And that Yankee bastard called her that to her face. Right out here on the street. In front of everyone. I told him we don't talk to our women like that, not even our fallen women. After that, there were a few words, and the next thing you know, we were fighting."

"You're like Don Quixote. Next thing you know, you'll be dueling with windmills," Dick said with a little chuckle.

"What? Who is Don Quixote?"

"Never mind. I was sorry to hear about Muley. When and where did it happen?"

"At Saylor Creek," Ron said. "You heard about all the others, didn't you?"

"Just that they had been killed. I don't know when, or where."

"Charley Konda was killed somewhere up in Missouri. Mickey Winters and Billy Votaw both died at Gettysburg. Perry Driscoll and the Blackburn boys were killed at Antietam. We thought you was killed at Franklin, till someone said you was just captured. I tried to sneak off 'n join, but Pa found out about it."

"Lord, Ron, be glad you didn't go," Dick said. "Believe me when I say there wasn't anything good to come out of that war."

A stagecoach arrived then, rolling rapidly down the main street accompanied by a clatter of hooves, the explosive snap of a whip, and the piercing whistle of its driver.

"Whoa! Whoa!" the driver called, hauling back on the reins and pushing against the brake lever with his right foot. The stage slid to a stop at the hotel just across the street. A moment later the door to the coach opened, and three well-dressed, paunchy men climbed down from the coach. They stepped behind the stage to wait by the boot while the driver pulled out their luggage.

"More damn carpetbaggers," Ron said, spitting in disgust.

"Carpetbaggers?"

"Yankees, come down here to steal what they can," Ron explained. "Folks call 'em carpetbaggers 'cause most of 'em bring a bag made out of carpet."

"What's there to steal? From what I hear, everyone is in a bad fix, what with the price of cattle and all."

"Yeah, and the Yankees want to keep it that way until they control all the land. The worst one of the bunch is a fella named Bryan Phelps. He has a business called Texas Land Development Company, and most of the carpetbaggers around here are working for him. Land development." Ron spat in disgust. "That's a good one. Land *stealing* is what it should be called. They're after every ranch in the valley and as soon as they get them, why, you just watch the market come back. Only then it'll be too late. We will have lost our place, and near 'bout ever'one else I know will have, too."

"How many head do you have over at your place?" Dick asked.

"I'm not sure. We had around a thousand, but last fall Pa and I drove a couple of hundred out into the range and turned 'em loose. We didn't have enough to feed them through the winter, and I couldn't kill them."

"You think you have five hundred left?"

Ron looked at Dick. "Five hundred? I reckon so. Why do you ask?"

"I plan to put together an outfit to take a herd up to the Dakota Territory. Why don't you throw in your five hundred and come with me? I've got a promise of forty dollars a head for every steer we can get there."

"Forty dollars a head?" Ron gasped. "My God, Dick that's a fortune. Yes, I'll go with you."

"Did you hear where I said we would be going?"

"Yeah, the Dakota Territory. I don't care, I want to go."

"We aren't talking a couple days on the trail, here, or even a couple of weeks. It's going to be one long, hard drive."

"Dick, at this point, I would soak my trousers in coal oil and drive a herd to hell to sell to the devil if he was payin' forty dollars a head. I don't aim to see our ranch wind up in the hands of the carpetbaggers if I can help it, and this just might be what I need to stop it."

"Funny you would mention the devil. In a way, selling our herd to the devil is just what we'll be doing."

"No matter, I'm with you. When do we start?"

"The sooner the better, but we're going to need a few more people."

"I'll get us some people, don't you worry about that." Ron started toward his horse.

"Ron?"

Ron turned back toward him.

"Any hands that you hire have to know that they won't be paid until we reach Dakota. And anyone who brings their own cows will have to put up their share of the supplies as well."

"Right. I'll tell 'em," Ron said.

Within two days, there were fifteen hundred cattle gathered in the north range of Trailback. The herd was composed of five hundred head from Trailback, five hundred from the Sietz Ranch, and five hundred from the Dumey Ranch. Chris Dumey, barely sixteen, had joined the outfit. In addition, there were two more young men, Moses Cohen and Dan Baker, who had hired on as hands. Dick explained the situation to them, telling them, among other things, that they wouldn't be paid until the herd was sold. In addition, they had to furnish their own horse, saddle, bedroll, and gun. But their food would be provided.

It didn't take long before word got around about Dick's plans. The news generated mixed reactions. There were some who hoped he was successful, believing that a market for cattle anywhere would help them. Most believed that it would end in failure. And there were the speculators, especially the carpetbaggers, who hoped that it would end in failure.

Bryan Phelps had the most interest in the

project. Phelps, who was forty years old, was an average-sized man who made up for a lack of hair by growing a heavy, black beard. During the war he had been a lieutenant colonel in the Fifth Ohio. His job was procurement officer, from which service he was discharged with honor and a letter of appreciation. What few realized was that he had used his position to enrich himself. In his capacity as procurement officer he had bought goods and products at low prices — not for the army, but for himself. He then resold those same supplies to the army for three to four times what he paid for them. By the end of the war, he was worth well over one hundred fifty thousand dollars and it was with those ill-begotten funds that he began building his land empire in West Texas.

Phelps' Texas Land Development Company occupied a building in what, before the war, had been a law office. The lawyer who had practiced from this location was killed at Seven Pines. The lawyer's widow sold the former law office to Bryan Phelps, and it soon became the cornerstone of Phelps' empire.

Dane Coleman came into the office and saw that Phelps was examining the map on the wall behind his desk. The map was of

Potter, Carson, Moore, and Hutchinson counties. Every ranch within that four-county area was clearly outlined, and the ranches Phelps had already bought were indicated by red cross-hatching. It took but a quick glance to see that more land was cross-hatched than wasn't. A closer examination, however, showed the problem Phelps was facing. In Hutchinson and Carson Country, there were four natural streams branching off from the Canadian River. These four streams — the Cottonwood, Limestone, Kirk, and Miranda — began on Trailback Ranch, making it the best-watered property in the entire panhandle.

It was because the other ranches were poorly watered that made them susceptible to Phelps' machinations. However, Phelps now faced the same problem they did. He had land, but there were certain times of the year when water could be a problem. Unless he got a dependable source of year-round water, he would always be limited as to the amount of livestock he could raise.

He had made Joel Konda an offer for his ranch, The Tilting K, and Konda indicated that he would take it, but the ranch Phelps really wanted was Trailback.

Hearing Coleman come in, Phelps turned

toward him. "What have you found out?" he asked.

"Looks like Hodson is going to go through with that crazy scheme of his to drive cattle to market up into the Dakota Territory. Or at least he's going to try," Coleman said. He walked over to point to the map. "Right now, he's got better than a thousand head gathered up here, in the north range of Trailback."

"If that young fool gets through with his herd, we never will get our hands on that ranch," Phelps said.

"I don't know what you are worrying about. There's no way he's going to get that herd through," Coleman said. "He's got over a thousand miles to go, and he's only got four men to help him." Coleman laughed. "If you can call them men. They're still wet-behind-the-ears yonkers."

"Sietz was man enough to handle that soldier the other day. Whipped him pretty good, from what I heard."

"He's young and strong. That won't mean anything when he's out on the trail."

Phelps took a step toward the map, then leaned in to examine it more closely. "Hmm, the north range, you say?"

"Yeah."

"Unless I'm mistaken, there's a draw that

runs from the old Springer Ranch, which I now own, down to about here." He traced an area on the map. "Comes right out on the north range of Trailback."

"Yeah, it does. Why? What do you have in mind?"

"I was just thinking," Phelps said. "If someone wanted to go from the Springer Ranch over to Trailback, they could probably get there without being seen."

Coleman smiled and stroked his chin. "Yeah," he said. "Yeah, I think they could do that real easy."

CHAPTER SIX

Somewhere in the predawn darkness a calf bawled anxiously, and its mother answered. In the distance a coyote sent up its long, lonesome wail, while out in the pond, frogs thrummed their night song. The moon was a thin crescent of silver, but the night was alive with stars, from the very bright all the way down to those not visible as individual bodies, but whose glow added to the luminous powder that dusted the distant sky.

Around the milling shapes of shadows that made up the small herd rode four young men: Ron Sietz, Chris Dumey, Moses Cohen, and Dan Baker.

The four young men were engaged in conversation.

"Ron, is it true that you got into a fight over Cassie Thomas?" Moses asked.

"Yeah."

" 'Cause someone called her a whore?"

"It wasn't just someone. It was some

Yankee son of a bitch. Cassie might be a whore, but she's one of our whores."

Moses chuckled. "You think she ain't sliding under the sheets for any Yankee who pays her?"

"She probably is. But that's not the point. The point is, she's a Southern whore, and the way I figure it, a Southern whore is equal to any Yankee lady."

Moses laughed. "You got a funny way of lookin' at things."

"Did you get anything for it?" Chris asked.

"What do you mean?"

"You know, did you get anything from Cassie? Like maybe a favor."

"I still don't know what you are talking about," Ron insisted.

"Chris means did Cassie let you lie with her," Moses explained.

"I didn't ask for the privilege."

"Have you ever been with her?" Chris asked.

"The cows seem a little restless," Ron said.

"Don't go changing the subject now," Chris said.

"Have you, or have you not, ever been with Cassie? Or any woman, for that matter?"

"Why are you so interested?" Ron asked.

Moses laughed. "I'll tell you why he's interested. It's 'cause he's still a virgin."

"Am not."

"Yes you are."

Chris was quiet for a moment. "Well, what if I am? I ain't always goin' to be. Fact is, I might just be visitin' Cassie myself before we start off on this trail drive. I figure now's about as good a time as any to get broke in."

"Well, Cassie's a good one for breaking you in, all right," Moses said.

"She is? How do you know? Moses, you've been with her? What's she like?"

"What do you mean, what is she like?"

"I mean, well, what's it like when you're with a woman?"

Ron, Moses, and Dan laughed.

"Stop laughing," Chris demanded.

"I'm sorry I'm laughing," Ron said. "But I just don't believe I would've told that."

"Told what?"

"That you've never been with a woman."

"Well, have *you* ever been with one?" Chris demanded.

"Like I said, I don't believe that's something I would tell," Ron answered.

"What about you, Dan?"

The calf's call for his mother came again,

this time with more insistence. The mother's answer had a degree of anxiousness to it.

"Sounds like one of 'em's wandered off," Dan said. "Maybe I'd better go find it."

"Hell, why bother? It'll find its own way back," Moses suggested.

"Maybe it will, and maybe it won't," Dan replied slapping his legs against the side of his horse. "But part of my job is to check it out." Dan rode off, disappearing into the darkness.

"Damn you, Dan, you just don't want to answer my question," Chris called after him. "Have you ever been with a woman, or haven't you?"

"Doesn't look to me like he's going to answer you," Ron said with a chuckle as they watched Dan disappear into the darkness.

Suddenly, from the darkness came a loud, bloodcurdling scream, filled with such terror that all three boys shivered all the way down to their boots.

"What the hell was that?" Ron asked.

"That sounded like Dan," Moses answered.

They heard the sound of galloping hooves, then saw Dan's horse appear out of the darkness, its nostrils flared wide, and its eyes wild with terror. It was moving at full gallop, the saddle empty.

"My God, where's Dan?" Chris asked.

Though the three men were wearing guns, none of them considered himself to be particularly skilled. Nevertheless, their friend was in trouble, and feeling the unfamiliar weight of pistols in their hands, the three boys rode into the darkness to his aid.

A moment later, gunshots erupted in the night, the muzzleflashes lighting up the herd.

"Jesus! What's happening? Who is it? They're all around us!" Moses shouted in terror, firing his gun wildly in the dark.

The three young men tried to fight back, but they were young, inexperienced, and scared. They saw shadows of mounted men in the darkness, briefly illuminated by the muzzle flashes of several gunshots. After a moment of intense gunfire the firing stopped, and it was silent except for the restless shuffle of the herd of cattle.

Ron sat in his saddle holding his smoking gun as he searched the night. He couldn't see anything now, because the brightness of the flashes had temporarily blinded his eyes.

"Chris?" he called softly. "Chris, do you see anything?"

"I've been shot," Chris's disembodied voice replied.

"Shot bad?"

"I don't know."

"Moses? Moses, you out there?"

Not getting an answer from Moses, he called Dan, though he knew he wouldn't hear anything from him.

"Dan . . . Moses? Answer me."

Ron heard the slow, measured beat of a horse coming toward him. Cocking his pistol, he pointed it toward the sound and waited. When the horse materialized out of the darkness, he saw Chris slumped in his saddle.

"Chris!" he shouted, riding quickly toward him.

"I've been shot," Chris said again.

When Ron's eyes had readjusted to the dark he saw Moses' horse close by.

Unlike Dan's horse, which had bolted in terror, Moses' horse had remained by his master. The horse was standing quietly over a body on the ground. Ron rode over quickly, then dismounted. It took only one glance to see that Moses was dead. Less than twenty feet away, he saw Dan's body as well. A few minutes earlier the four young cowboys had been talking and laughing. Now two of them were dead and one was wounded.

"Is he dead?" Chris asked.

"Yes. Both of them are."

"Who did this?" Chris asked. "I never even saw anyone."

"I don't know," Ron answered. Frustrated, he called out. "Who are you? Who's out there? What do you want?"

He heard nothing in response but the continuing shuffle of the cattle and the moan of a ceaseless wind.

"Ron, I want to go home," Chris said. "Right now."

Ron thought about the herd and wondered about leaving them unattended long enough to take Chris home. Whoever did this might be cattle rustlers and if he left now, they would take the herd. Then he realized that if they wanted the herd, there was nothing he could do to stop them now, anyway. Besides, why would anyone want to steal the herd? At the current market price, cattle wasn't worth stealing.

"All right, Chris. I'll get you home," Ron said, riding over to take the reins of his friend's horse.

Not more than a few hundred yards away from Ron and Chris, a short, but powerfully built man sat on his horse with his hat pulled low over a bald head and browless eyes. Though he had put everything in motion, he had not personally taken part in the proceedings. Now one of the other men, with the smell of death still in his nostrils, rode up to him.

"That's it, Coleman," the rider said. "We kilt two of 'em and I think we hit one of the others. You want us to go back and kill them, too?"

"No," Coleman said, holding up his hand. "Chances are you got 'em both so scared now that they peed in their britches. And once they start talkin' about it, why, Hodson won't be able to get anyone else to go with him. And he sure as hell ain't goin' to try to take the herd up to Dakota all by himself," Coleman snorted. "No, sir. I think this trail drive is over."

"It could've been anyone," the sheriff suggested the next day, when Dick went into town to report the murderous raid of the night before. "You know how things are right now, what with all those soldiers coming home from the war."

Dick shook his head. "No, I don't believe that. I can't imagine any returning soldiers doing anything like that, whether they be Yanks or Rebs," he said. "What would be the reason for it? Besides, most of the soldiers I know have had enough killing."

"I wouldn't think these fellas would be regulars," the sheriff said. "More'n likely they're from one of them irregular units. They say Quantrill's still alive somewhere and up to no good."

"Sheriff, even men like that wouldn't kill without a reason. They would kill to steal money, or a horse, perhaps. These people took nothing."

"Maybe they were just hungry and wanted a couple of beeves."

"You know as well as I do that there are cows wandering the range now. If anyone is hungry they don't need to steal a cow. They can go out into the bush and find one."

"Well, if you don't think it's anything like that, I don't have the slightest idea who might have done such a thing," the sheriff said.

"Don't you?" Dick challenged.

The sheriff frowned. "What do you mean by that?"

"Sheriff, who doesn't want me to make this drive?"

"A lot of people don't want you to make this drive. Including, I've heard, your parents."

"Bryan Phelps doesn't want it most of all."

"Couldn't be Phelps," the sheriff said. "There was a church dinner last night, and Phelps was there from beginning to end. I know, because I was there, too, and I saw him."

"If Phelps didn't do it himself, he had someone do it for him," Dick said.

"You'd better watch talk like that, Hodson, it could get you into trouble," the sheriff said. "You can't go around making accusations unless you have some evidence to back it up."

"I have two dead riders," Dick said. "Isn't that evidence enough?"

"Not unless you have an eyewitness who can testify as to who did it."

"It was too dark. Neither Ron nor Chris saw anything."

"Then I've got no reason to suspect Bryan Phelps."

"All right, maybe you don't have enough evidence to arrest him," Dick said. "But I can't believe that you don't even suspect him."

"As far as I know, Bryan Phelps is an honest businessman. He's come here to make a home for himself, Dick. Seems to me like we're never going to get over this war unless we can get along with people like that."

"You get along with him, Sheriff," Dick said. "I'm going out to the Dumey place to check on Chris."

"How bad was he hurt?"

"Not too bad. He was shot in the arm," Dick said.

"You give the Dumeys my regards, will you?" the sheriff said. Leaning back in his chair, he picked up a newspaper and began to read, not even looking up as Dick stormed out of his office.

Just as Dick started to untie his horse from the hitching rail, someone called out to him.

"You Dick Hodson?"

Dick looked around to see a stout, bald-headed man. Because the man had no noticeable neck nor facial hair of any kind, including eyebrows, his head looked like a cannonball, balanced on his shoulders.

"Yeah, I'm Dick Hodson. Who wants to know?"

"The name is Coleman. Dane Coleman. Mr. Phelps wants to see you."

"What about?"

"He wants to make you a proposition."

"I'm not interested."

Dick heard a gun being cocked, and when he looked behind him, he saw another man, holding a pistol leveled at him.

"Mr. Phelps would really like to talk to you," Coleman said.

Dick shrugged his shoulders. "Well, if you put it like that, how can I refuse?"

Dick refused the cigar Phelps offered him.

"This isn't exactly a friendly visit," he said. "I was brought here under the point of a gun."

Phelps frowned. "Morgan, put that away," he said. "What do you mean threatening Mr. Hodson like that?"

Morgan looked confused. "But Mr. Phelps, you said you wanted to see him."

"Yes, I wanted to *see* him, not *threaten* him. Now, put it away."

"Yes, sir," Morgan said, meekly, sheathing his pistol.

"My most sincere apologies, Mr. Hodson," Phelps said. "I would like to talk to you, but it wasn't my intention to have you brought here like this." He indicated the door with a wave of his arm. "By all means, you are free to go."

Looking just over Phelps' shoulder, Dick could see the large map on the wall. He was curious about the cross-hatching until he realized that these must be the ranches Phelps had already bought.

"As long as I'm here, I'll stay to see what you have to say," Dick said.

"Good," Phelps said. He saw where Dick was looking, then he pointedly stepped out of the way to afford Dick an unobstructed view of the entire map. "You seem to have an interest in the holdings of

Texas Land Development."

"You own all those ranches?" Dick had no idea Phelps had been so successful in his acquisitions.

"Yes."

"How?"

"Many of them I bought from the previous owner," Phelps said. "If he was smart, he sold directly to me and managed to come away from the deal with a little money. If he held on too long, he wound up losing his ranch for taxes. Then I was able to take possession for pennies an acre . . . none of which went to the previous owner."

"Phelps, I hope you didn't bring me here to make an offer for Trailback," Dick said. "Because it isn't for sale."

"I haven't made an offer for Trailback yet, because despite your father's condition, it is a little stronger than most of the other ranches."

"What do you know about my father's condition?"

"I know he is no longer able to work his land."

"He doesn't have to work it. I'm back now."

"Yes, you are. But as I understand it you are about to undertake a foolish adventure. I haven't been misinformed, have I? You are planning on moving a herd of cattle to the Dakota Territory?"

"I am."

Phelps shook his head. "I would think, particularly given your father's condition, that you would be more interested in staying home and looking after the ranch."

"There is no cattle market here."

Phelps shook his head. "Yes, that's true, isn't it?" he replied. "But there was a cattle market before the war, and there will be another soon. In fact, I predict that the market will be booming. The people in the north were cut off from a steady supply of beef for too long. They'll be wanting to put steaks on their table again, and those steaks will have to come from somewhere."

"And you are getting into position to supply that market," Dick said. It was a statement, not a question.

"Yes, I am. And the market can be there for anyone else who has the patience to wait for it."

"It isn't patience that is required, Phelps, and you know it. Those of us who wait will have to have money — money to live on, money to improve the land, and, most of all, money to pay the taxes."

"Yes, that is true."

"And that is why I'm going to Dakota."

"Suppose you found a market here for your cattle. Would you sell them?"

"You know of such a market?"

Phelps nodded. "Now that I have the land, it is time I started investing in cattle. You don't need to go to Dakota to sell your herd. Sell it to me, right here, right now."

Dick looked at Phelps through narrowed eyes. "What are you offering?"

"Well, since there are cattle wandering the range, cattle to be had simply by rounding them up, you can understand that I don't expect to pay much. However, as you already rounded up your beeves, I look at buying your herd as a matter of convenience. I'll give you fifty cents a head."

"What? You must be crazy!"

Phelps chuckled. "I didn't think you would go for that, but you can't blame me for trying. I'll give you ten dollars a head for them. They're only paying twenty-five dollars a head in Chicago, right now."

"You're paying ten dollars a head? That's actually quite generous under the circumstances," Dick said. "But I don't understand. I was led to believe there was no market at all. That's not close to what it was before the war but, if you're paying ten dollars a head, most of these people should have been able to save their ranches." Dick took in the cross-hatched ranches on Phelps' map.

Phelps laughed. "It is a generous offer," he said. "So generous in fact, that I've never made it to anyone else. And the offer isn't being extended to anyone else now. It is only for you."

"I see. To keep me from going to Dakota?"

"Yes."

"At the moment, only half the herd belongs to me."

"That doesn't matter. I'll pay ten dollars a head for every animal that joins your herd."

Dick stroked his chin. "Let me think about your offer for a while," he said.

"Of course. But don't take too long. I don't intend to leave the offer on the table indefinitely."

Chapter Seven

Leaving Phelps' office, Dick rode out to the Dumey Ranch to check on Chris. To his relief he was in excellent condition. The bullet hadn't gone through his arm, but had merely creased it. The wound wasn't much more than an abrasion, as if he had ridden into a tree branch.

"All right, so he wasn't hurt bad this time. But he and Ron was just lucky, that's all. Them other two boys was killed," Josh Dumey said. Josh was Chris' father. "Now I lost me one boy at Shiloh. I ain't aimin' to lose another. Chris ain't goin'."

"Pa, I want to go. I ain't scared none. Besides, we need to sell those cows. If we don't, we ain't goin' to make it," Chris complained.

"You're only sixteen years old, boy. You ain't goin', and that's that," Josh said. He looked at Dick. "If you want to take the five hundred head with you and sell 'em, why you go right ahead. I'll give you a commission on ever' one you sell, but my boy ain't goin' with you."

"I appreciate your offer, Mr. Dumey," Dick replied. "But if I can't get anymore men to help me with the drive, then I can't take any more cows. It's going to be hard enough to handle what I've already got." He made no mention of Phelps' offer to buy all the cows in his herd for ten dollars a head, because he knew that Dumey would jump at the chance.

"You want my advice? Don't even try it," Josh Dumey said. "There wasn't that many Hutchinson or Carson County boys who come back from the war. Speakin' as someone who lost a son, I say we don't want to lose anymore. Before you start off on a fool venture like this, think of your mama and daddy and think of the mammas and daddies of anyone crazy enough to go with you."

"I am thinking of them, Mr. Dumey," Dick said. "If I can take a herd to Dakota and sell it for forty dollars a head, that's going to force the market up everywhere. That can only help the ranchers who are still hanging on. On the other hand, if I stand by and do nothing, then all those boys who died, all those sons, would have died for nothing."

Dumey was quiet for a moment, then he nodded and put his hand on Dick's shoulder. "It's good what you are trying to do, boy," he said. "And I wish you luck with it. But please, don't ask me for Chris. He's all I have left."

"I understand, Mr. Dumey," Dick said. "I won't take him, and I won't hold it against you for keeping him back."

Turning away from the disappointed look in Chris' face, Dick walked back out to his horse for the long ride back to his own ranch.

"Josh Dumey is right," Dick's mother said after hearing what had transpired. "I just wish I could keep you from going the way he's keeping Chris from going."

"You don't mean that, Ma."

"Yes, I do mean it. Think about it, Dick. You've just come back to us. I can't bear to think of you leaving us again."

"It's only for a few months, Ma. Only until I get the cows delivered."

"It's too dangerous. What if something happens to you?"

"Whatever is going to happen is going to happen," Dick replied. "Moses Cohen and Dan Baker were killed right here on our own place. Where you are doesn't matter."

"That's exactly what I mean," Delia said. "That just shows you how dangerous this whole thing is."

"Of course it's dangerous. We are fighting a war for our survival here, and any war is dangerous. But I have to do it, Ma. I have to get this herd delivered to Fort Sully."

"And how do you plan on doing that?" Dick's father asked. "With just you and Ron Sietz?"

"I don't know exactly. But I am going to do it. I'd like to think I was doing it with your blessing."

John sighed, then put his hand on his son's shoulder. "You've got my blessing," he said.

"John, you can't mean that!" Delia said.

"I do mean it, Delia. If I hadn't had this seizure, I'd be going with him."

"Thanks, Pa."

"You're going to need a wagon," John said. "We've got three, but none of them are fit for a journey like this. But if we take the axle off one, and the tongue and double-tree off another, we just might be able to put one together that will get the job done."

"Good idea."

"Come on, let's take a look at them," John invited. As he started toward the front door Dick thought he noticed a new animation in his step. Delia noticed it, too, and she reached out to take her son by the arm.

"Look at him. I haven't seen him this spry since before the apoplexy. I think the old fool really would go with you if he had half a chance. Promise me you won't take him."

Dick smiled. "I promise."

"And you'll be careful?"

"I'll be very careful."

"Then go. With your mother's blessing, go."

Dick took his mother in his arms, then kissed her on the forehead.

"Dick, get out here," his father called. "I don't aim to put this wagon together all by myself."

An hour later, Dick had the best bed of the three wagons up on blocks. The wheels and axles had been removed, and he was about to replace them with the front axle from a second wagon and the rear axle from a third.

"There's a rider comin'," John said.

"Who is it? Ron?" Dick was on his back under the wagon bed, bolting an axle guide into place.

"I don't think so," John said. Then after a moment he said, "Well, I'll be. It's the Konda girl."

"The Konda girl? You mean Marline? Charley's little sister? What's she doing over here?"

"Could be she's just stopping by to say hello," John said. "You know, you and her brother were awfully close."

Dick scooted out from under the wagon bed, then washed his hands in a nearby bucket of water. He was drying them on a piece of burlap when Marline rode up to the front of the barn and dismounted.

Dick's first reaction was one of surprise. Marline had been just over fifteen the last time he saw her. She was a skinny, tomboyish thing who was always in the way. She wasn't skinny now, and if she was still tomboyish, it certainly didn't show. Marline Konda had turned into an exceptionally pretty woman.

"Hello, Marline," Dick greeted.

"Hi, Dick. Welcome home," Marline said.

"It's good to be back," Dick said. He pointed toward the house. "I think Ma has some lemonade made. Would you like a glass?"

"Yes, that would be nice, thank you."

Dick walked with her to the house, where she was greeted warmly by Dick's mother. Then, taking a couple of glasses of lemonade, they moved out to the gazebo.

"It's been a while since you and I sat here together," Dick suggested.

Marline laughed. "We never sat together, Dick Hodson. You ran me away every chance you got. As I recall, you and Charley considered me a pest."

Dick laughed, too. "As I recall, Marline, you were a pest," he said.

For the next several minutes, the two young people talked about old times. Marline told him everything the family knew about Charley's death.

"He was with General Sterling Price," she said. "He was killed somewhere near a town called Rolla. It wasn't much of a battle, and the Confederates were forced from the field so fast that they were barely able to take their wounded. The dead were left behind, to be buried by the Yankees. Charley is up there, in one of those unmarked graves, but we don't have any idea which one is his."

"I know how the Yankee burial parties worked," Dick said. "If he had anything at all to identify him, they would have a record of where he is." He went on to explain that the reason he knew about the Yankee burial parties was because he had been left for dead, and a Yankee burial party had not only found him but had, in fact, saved his life. Then he briefly told her of his subsequent time in the Yankee prison camp.

"Dick, is it true that you are going to take a herd up to the Dakota Territory?" Marline asked when there was a lull in the conversation.

"Yes," Dick said.

"And you are going to sell the herd to Yankees for forty dollars a head?"

"Yes."

"I want to go with you."

"What?"

"I heard that any rancher who furnishes their own horse, saddle, bedroll, gun, and food, can put five hundred head of their own cattle into the herd and come with you. I want to do that."

"Oh, Marline, I don't know," Dick said.

"You don't know? Is there something I forgot?"

"This is going to be a long, hard, and dangerous drive," Dick said.

"I wouldn't expect it to be a picnic."

"What I mean is, it's much too hard for a woman."

"Dick Hodson, I can ride as well as any man," Marline said. "And better than most. You should know that. I beat you enough times when we were younger. And I can shoot, too. As I have also proven to you."

"Those were games, Marline. This is real."

"Dick, I stopped playing games the day all the men went away to war. There were no men to hunt down the strays, handle the round ups, brand the calves, put out the hay in the winter when the snow was waist deep, shoot wolves in the springtime when they were attacking the herds, roof the barn, and fight off Indians. Who do you think did it?"

"I'm sure you had to do things that you didn't expect, but . . ."

"I wasn't the only one," Marline interrupted. "On every ranch where only women remained, we did the jobs the men would have done, had they been here."

Dick shook his head. "I don't understand why you would even want to go," he said.

"That should be obvious. Why are you going? To sell your cattle for enough money to save your ranch. Right?"

"Yes."

"I want to go for the same reason."

Dick was silent for a moment. "I can see that," he finally said.

Marline smiled broadly. "Then you'll let me go with you?"

"No," Dick said. "I won't do that, but I will take five hundred head from your ranch and sell them for you."

"Are you doing that for anyone else?"

"No. I can't do it for anyone else. Right

now there's only Ron Sietz and myself. We're going to be hard-pressed as it is. We can't take on anymore cattle."

"Including mine," Marline said.

"No, I said I would take yours, and I will. I owe it to Charley."

"Never mind," Marline said. "If I don't go, my cattle don't go."

"Marline, be sensible. Even if I said you could go with me, do you think your mother and father would let you go?"

"I'm twenty years old, Dick Hodson," Marline said. "I don't need my parents' permission any more than you do."

Dick thought about how just a few hours earlier, he had asked his parents not for their permission but for their blessing. He had already determined that he was going to go no matter what they said or did, so he could understand Marline's determination. For a moment he almost relented and said she could go with him. But before he could form the words, he had second thoughts. What if it had been Marline killed the other night, instead of Moses or Dan? That thought gave him pause, and he stuck by his original decision.

"I'm sorry, Marline," he said, shaking his head. "I just can't let you go."

"Thank your mother for the lemonade,"

Marline said, setting the glass down. She stood.

"You don't have to run off so quickly," Dick said. "I was enjoying our visit."

"You were working when I arrived," Marline said, coolly. "I wouldn't want to keep you."

"Marline, don't be like that," Dick said as he followed her toward her horse. "You know I can't take you. I can't really believe you even asked."

"Goodbye, Dick," Marline said. Mounting her animal, she turned it quickly then galloped across the lot.

Instead of going around the hedgerow at the far end of the lot, she urged her horse over it. The animal and rider cleared the hedgerow as gracefully as if they were performing ballet. Dick knew she was doing it to impress him, and he had to admit that she did.

CHAPTER EIGHT

Dick was surprised the next day when he saw several head of cattle being pushed onto Trailback's pastures. Riding out to see what was going on, he saw a small, wiry young man, whistling and shouting as he drove the herd. He was riding one horse and leading another.

When the young man saw Dick he rode toward him, touching the brim of his hat as he reached him. The young man's hat was oversized, with a particularly high crown, almost as if he was trying to use it to make up for his small stature.

"You the fella they call Dick Hodson?" he asked.

"I am."

The boy smiled and stuck out his hand. "The name's Corbin. Buck Corbin. I come to join you," he said.

"Buck, don't get the wrong idea here, but how old are you?" Buck didn't look a day over fourteen.

"I'm eighteen," Buck replied. "But if that's not old enough for you, tell me just how old you want me to be and I'll accommodate you."

Dick laughed at the answer, then nodded toward the cows. "You bring these yourself?"

"I did."

"Corbin, you say? I don't know any Corbins. What ranch are you riding for?"

"I'm ridin' for my own ranch," Buck said.

"Your own ranch?"

"It's mine now. My Pa didn't come back from the war," Buck said simply. "There's just me and my ma livin' there."

"Where would this ranch be?"

"North Moore County."

Dick whistled. "That's a good fifty miles from here. How long did it take you to get here?"

"Left yesterday mornin', bedded them down on the range last night, and pushed them on in here today."

"Well, Buck, if you can bring this many head that far all by yourself, then I reckon you would be the kind of man I'd like to have with me. You're welcome to come along."

"Thanks. Where do I put these critters?"

"Take 'em out to the north range, join them

with the others you see there, and wait there."

"What am I waitin' on?"

"For the others."

"How many others will there be?"

"I can't tell you that. I don't have any idea. Right now there are three of us."

"Just three?"

"That's right."

Buck stroked his chin. "How far is it up to this place we're goin'?"

"Better than a thousand miles."

"There's just three men to push a herd one thousand miles?"

"Looks that way right now. Unless the thought scares you and you want to back out. Then there'll just be two of us."

"You think two of you could make that drive?"

"Unless Ron backs out as well," Dick said. "Then that would leave just one. Me."

"What would you do then?"

"Friend, I'm taking my cows to Dakota if I have to tie a rope around them and pull them up there."

"All by yourself?"

"If that's the way it is, yes. All by myself."

Buck chuckled. "Well, it ain't ever goin' to get to that," he said. "I've come this far, and I figure I'll be goin' with you, even if it's no more than the two of us."

"You'll be welcome."

"When are we leavin'?"

"Tomorrow," Dick said. "Or maybe the day after. No later."

Buck twisted around in his saddle and reached back toward the horse he was leading. A pair of gunnysacks were hanging across the animal's back.

"I got bacon, beans, flour, sugar, coffee, and rice in here," he said. "Fact is, I got much more'n I'll need. Figured I'd throw it in with your possibles."

"Good. We've got a wagon," Dick said. "No driver yet," he added with a chuckle. "But we do have a wagon."

The prospect of there being only three of them disappeared when Dooley Winters showed up that afternoon, driving five hundred head of his own cattle. Dooley, the younger brother of Mickey Winters, was nineteen. Mickey had been one of Dick's closest friends before the war, but Mickey, like so many other boys from the Panhandle, had been killed.

Dooley was tall and thin. He had always supposed that his older brother would inherit the ranch and therefore never really developed that much of an affinity for the cow business. It was Dooley's intention to become a lawyer, and he had already begun his studies. In fact he was carrying several books with him in his saddlebag even now, including three volumes of law, a history book, a book on grammar, and a couple of novels.

"Dooley, you sure you want to go through with this?" Dick asked.

"I don't have any choice," Dooley said. "If we can't make any money from these cows, we'll be losing our place for taxes next year."

"No offense meant, but I never really looked at you as a rancher. I mean, even when we were young, you didn't seem to care much for it."

"I still don't care that much for it," Dooley admitted. "But with Mickey gone, the mantle has fallen upon my shoulders."

"All right, take your herd to the north range. You'll see two men there. Ron Sietz you already know. The other fella is Buck Corbin, from Moore County. By the way, don't let Buck's looks deceive you. He may be small, but I've got a feeling he's tough as a bobcat."

At the Konda Ranch

"What time will your friends be over for the quilting?" Trudy Konda asked her daughter.

"Early this afternoon," Marline answered. "Sometime around one o'clock."

"Are you still working on the star pattern?"

"Yes, Mama."

"Land o' Goshen, how long have you been working on that same quilt?"

"It's been about two years since we started it," Marline answered.

"Two years! Any other quilting group would have been finished months ago. The problem is, you girls do a lot more talking than you do quilting."

"Well of course we do, but that's the fun of it," Marline defended.

Trudy chuckled. "I agree. Quilting with your friends is, and always has been, an excuse for us women to visit and talk." She walked into the parlor, where earlier, Marline had laid out the quilt. "And I must admit you and your friends are doing a wonderful job. The quilt is beautiful."

"Thanks, Mama."

Marline and her three girlfriends had developed an intricate design of white stars, outlined in red against a blue field. The stars were brought out in relief by cotton padding. The girls had also embroidered their name and date of birth in each of the four corners of the quilt.

Marline's three friends were Anita Votaw, Kitty Blackburn, and Priscilla Driscoll. At twenty, Marline was the oldest of the group and also their leader. The others had all agreed, however, that Marline would probably have been their leader regardless of their relative ages.

"The needlework is exquisite. Your grandmother would have been very proud of you to see something like this," Trudy said as she ran her fingers along the texture of the quilt. "Have you decided whose quilt it will be yet?"

"It is going to go to the first one of us to get married."

"Well, now, that sounds like a sensible idea, especially as you are the oldest and will probably marry first," Trudy replied.

"And just who am I to marry, Mama? There aren't many eligible young men left."

"Sadly enough, that's the truth of it," Trudy replied. "Dick Hodson came back from the war. He's game in one leg, but I don't think it's slowed him down that much. And, as I recall, you always rather liked him."

"I do like him, but Dick and Charley were together so much that I was never able to think of him as anything but a brother."

"He isn't your brother."

"I know," Marline said.

"But, you are probably right not to consider him. I hear he has some crazy idea about taking a herd of cows all the way up to Dakota to try and sell them."

"Maybe it's not such a crazy idea," Marline said.

"It's about the most foolish idea I've ever heard of," Trudy said. "He should be here, helping his father. The poor man hasn't been himself ever since his bout with apoplexy."

"I'm sure that he believes that taking the cattle to a market where he can get a fair price is helping his father."

"Yes, well, there's nothing to be gained by talking about it, since it's none of our worry. Especially now that your father has made up his mind to sell the ranch. Listen, dear, I won't be here when your friends arrive. Your father is going to help Caleb Blackburn patch the roof on his house, and I promised Roberta that I would help her with a dress she is making. But there are some cookies and lemonade in the kitchen for you and your friends."

"Thanks, Mama," Marline replied. "I'll walk out front to see you off."

When Joel brought the buckboard around, Marline hugged her mother tightly.

"Goodbye, Mama," she said. Then she took her father by the hand. "Goodbye, Papa. You all take care."

"What's gotten into you, girl?" Joel asked gruffly. "We're just goin' over to the Blackburn place. We'll be back by suppertime."

"I just . . . wanted to tell you goodbye, is all," Marline said. She watched them drive off, remaining on the front porch until the buckboard and team could barely be seen. Not until then did she let the tears come.

By the time Anita and Kitty arrived half an hour later, Marline was no longer crying. It wouldn't do to let them see her tears, especially as she had been the instigator and principal advocate of what they were now calling "the big adventure."

Anita was a small girl with dark hair and flashing eyes, and though she was barely five feet tall, she was every inch a woman. She was nearly as skilled a horsewoman as Marline, and was good with a rifle. But Anita's particular talent lay in her ability to function outdoors. She seemed to have an innate feel for the lay of the land, could find water almost as if she could smell it, and could track anything. Anita credited her outdoor skills to her grandmother, who was full-blooded Comanche.

Kitty was tall and willowy, with light brown hair, blue eyes, and a spray of freckles across her nose. Kitty, who was the most studious of the group, had taught school since she was sixteen. Her secret desire — which she had shared with no one, not even her closest friends — was to write a book some day. To that end she kept a secret journal, trying to find some time each day to put down a few thoughts.

Last to arrive was Priscilla Driscoll. Priscilla was a tall, strongly built woman who feared neither man nor beast. Well proportioned, she was attractive to many men, but only to those men who weren't intimidated by her size, strength, and demeanor. In a time when social decorum suggested that women should be shy and withdrawn, Priscilla was anything but.

The four girls went into the parlor, but they didn't work on the quilt.

"I rode out to Elder Canyon this morning to check on the herd. It's all there. Any of your families miss the cattle yet?"

"My pa hasn't noticed anything," Anita said.

"Mine, either," Kitty added.

"Good here," Priscilla said.

"And you are sure none of you have said anything to anyone about what we are doing?" Marline asked.

Anita and Priscilla both assured Marline that they had said nothing, but Kitty didn't respond.

"Kitty?" Marline asked suspiciously.

Kitty paused for a moment before she replied. "I haven't said anything to anyone," she finally said. "But . . ." she let the sentence hang.

"But what?"

"Marline, there is no way we will be back by the time school starts in the fall, and that worries me. What about the children?"

"What about them?"

"They'll need a teacher."

"Kitty, if we don't save our ranches, there won't be a need for a teacher, because there won't be any kids left to go to school. Everyone will be forced to move out of the county."

"Still, to just leave without any word," Kitty said. "It doesn't seem right."

"Once we are gone, and our families start talking to each other, I think they will figure out what has happened," Marline said. "Especially after they see that some of the cattle are missing. Now, are you with us or not?"

Kitty looked into the faces of her three closest friends, reading in their expressions support and a plea that she stay with them. She smiled.

"I'm with you," she said. "In fact, I've already packed everything I will need."

"Same here," Anita said.

"Me, too," Priscilla put in.

"Now, what about guns? And ammunition? Do you have that?"

The three girls nodded.

"I hope we aren't making a foolish mistake in doing this drive all by ourselves. Because I'll tell you one thing that's bothering me. Even if we get there, we won't have any idea where to go with the cattle. There are thousands of square miles of totally uninhabited land in the Dakota Territory. If we aren't in the right place at the right time, we'll be stuck with the herd."

"It's not *if* we get there, it's *when* we get there," Marline corrected. "And as for going alone? I'm perfectly prepared to if we have to, because I think we can do it. But as I explained, the plan is to join up with Dick Hodson's outfit in about a week."

"Oh, I understand the plan," Kitty said. "But what if Dick Hodson doesn't? What if he won't let us join him?"

Marline sighed. "I won't lie to you," she said, "that's the fly in the ointment. I'm not sure he *will* let us. But we'll be well on our way by then, so that will prove to him we can do it. And since each of us are only putting two hundred and fifty head into the herd, he'll be doubling his outfit without doubling his herd. I believe by that time he'll welcome the extra hands."

"And if he doesn't?" Anita asked.

"If he doesn't? Why, we'll just trail along with him anyway!" Marline said.

"What if he throws us off?" Kitty asked.

"Hah! I'd like to see him try," Priscilla said, putting her hands on her hips and assuming a belligerent posture.

"You I'm not worried about," Anita said. "You couldn't be moved with a team of mules. But all he would have to do to get rid of me is wave his hands. He doesn't even have to touch me — the wind waving from his hand would blow me away."

The others laughed heartily.

"This is it, ladies," Marline said, sticking her hand out. "After this, there is no turning back."

One by one the others reached out to take her hand until soon, the four arms formed a star, not unlike the ones they had sewn into the quilt.

CHAPTER NINE

Six Days Later, on the Range

The first pink fingers of dawn touched the sagebrush, and the light was soft, and the air was cool. Dick liked the range best early in the morning. The herd was now four days on the trail. Four days and as yet, no problems except fatigue. Driving cattle, even a relatively small herd of only two thousand cows, was almost more than four men could handle.

The last morning star made a bright pinpoint of light over the purple hills that lay in a ragged line to the north and west. The coals from the campfire of the night before were still glowing, and Dick threw chunks of wood onto them then stirred the fire into crackling flames that danced merrily against the bottom of the suspended coffee pot.

A rustle of wind through feathers caused him to look up just in time to see a golden eagle diving on its prey. The eagle swooped

113

back into the air carrying a tiny field mouse, which kicked fearfully in the eagle's claws. A rabbit bounded quickly back into its hole, frightened by the sudden appearance of the eagle.

Dick poured himself a cup of coffee and sat down to enjoy it. It was black and steaming, and he had to blow on it before he could suck it through his lips. He watched the sun's rays peek over the horizon, then stream brightly down onto the open range land.

Ron had taken a ride around the herd, and Dick heard his horse coming back in.

"I tell you, that coffee smells awful good," Ron said, swinging down from his saddle and walking toward the fire, rubbing his hands together eagerly. "I wouldn't mind havin' a biscuit, either."

"I put some in the Dutch oven a few minutes ago," Dick said. "They'll be ready in a minute or two." He looked over at a couple of lumps on the ground. The lumps were actually bedrolls, and right now both were occupied. "I guess I'd better wake up Buck and Dooley."

"No, let me do it," Ron said. "They seemed to take particular pleasure in waking me up last night at midnight when it was time for us to take the watch. I'm going to enjoy returning the favor."

"Be my guest," Dick invited.

Ron crept over very quietly until he was positioned exactly between the two sleeping men. He stood there for a moment, listening to their soft snoring as he smiled in anticipation of the moment. Then he yelled at the top of his voice, "All right you two, off your asses and on your feet! Out of those sacks and into the heat! Up and at 'em, boys, we're burnin' sunlight!"

Buck and Dooley sat up as quickly as if they had been popped up by a spring, Dooley letting out a little shout of surprise as he did so.

Buck groaned. "Damn, you, Ron! From the way you were carrying on, I thought the cattle were stampeding."

"No, no, nothing like that, boys. Dick made biscuits, and I just wanted you to be able to enjoy them while they're still hot."

"I tell you what I would like to do with those biscuits while they're still hot," Buck grumbled.

That Evening, on the Trail

Marline couldn't recall when she had been so tired. It was a bone-aching, back-breaking tired, and yet there was an exhilaration that transcended the tiredness. The exhilaration came from the excitement of the drive and from the feeling of doing something that would help her family.

Marline knew that by now her family, the Driscolls, Blackburns, and Votaws, had long ago pieced together enough information to realize what had happened. There would be exactly two hundred and fifty head of cattle missing from each of the ranches, and the girls' clothes would be gone. Also, the best horse had been taken from each ranch.

For the first few days of the drive Marline expected to see her father coming after her at any moment, demanding that she return home. She hoped he didn't, because she had already made up her mind that she wasn't going back no matter how much he might demand it. On the other hand, though they would never have approved of such an adventure outright, Marline was beginning to think that by not coming after them, the four sets of parents were tacitly giving their approval.

Marline wasn't the only one who was feeling the excitement of the drive. She could see it in the eyes and on the faces of the other girls as well. The excitement was infectious and self-feeding and seemed to grow as the drive progressed. It was all around them, like the smell of the air before a spring shower, or the smell of woodsmoke on a crisp fall day.

But it wasn't fall or spring. It was summer, and throughout the long, hot days the sun beat relentlessly down on the girls and the animals below. Mercifully, by the time the herd reached a place where it could be halted for the night, the yellow glare of the early summer sky had mellowed into the steel blue of late afternoon, and the girls were refreshed with a breath of cool air.

To the west, the sun dropped all the way to the foothills while to the east purple shadows, like bunches of violets, gathered in the notches and timbered draws. Behind the setting sun, great bands of color spread out along the horizon. Those few clouds that dared to intrude on this perfect day glowed orange in the darkening sky.

"Marline, supper's ready," Kitty called, interrupting Marline's contemplation of the beautiful sunset.

"My that looks good, Kitty," Priscilla said, checking out the fare. "You're going to make some man a fine wife some day," she said as she began filling her plate. "In fact, if I were a man, I'd marry you myself."

★ ★ ★ ★ ★

It was after midnight.

Marline didn't know why she couldn't go to sleep. She certainly was tired enough, but no matter how many times she turned and repositioned herself, sleep continued to elude her. She sat up in her blankets and looked over at Priscilla. The soft snores emanating from Priscilla's lips showed that she was having no trouble at all.

Marline wondered what time it was. With only four of them, they had divided the night duty in half, changing shifts at midnight. Marline and Priscilla had taken the first shift. Kitty and Anita were riding nighthawk now and would do so until daybreak. At daybreak they would normally have breakfast, then start driving the cows north again. At least that had been the routine until today. Today they would stay put.

Upon leaving Hutchinson County, the women had taken a different route from Dick Hodson's outfit. They followed a course that would cross trails with the men approximately one week out. If their plot was correct, they had now reached the place where the two routes would intersect.

Marline and the others left twenty-four hours ahead of the men so they would be in position before the Hodson outfit arrived. They had planned for a week's separation so the rendezvous would be far enough north that Dick Hodson's hand would be forced, and he couldn't send them back. The only question now was if they had made it here in time, and Marline prayed that they had.

With sleep still unattainable, Marline got up and saddled her horse in hopes that a ride around the herd would make her sleepy.

After a minute or two, Marline was far away from the camp, swallowed up by the blue velvet of night. The night air caressed her skin like fine silk, and it carried on its breath the scent of pear cactus flowers. Overhead the moon was a brilliant silver orb, and stars glistened like diamonds. In the distance, mountain peaks rose in great and mysterious dark slabs against the midnight sky. Marline was aware of the quiet herd, with cows standing motionless in rest. An owl landed close by, his wings making a soft whirring sound. The owl looked at Marline with big round, glowing eyes, as if he had been made curious by her unexpected presence.

Marline rode quietly for several moments until she came to a small grass-covered knoll. Here, she heard a splashing, bubbling sound, and she knew that it was the same, swiftly flowing stream had caused them to choose this spot as the place to wait for Dick Hodson's herd to join them.

Marline got off her horse and walked to the top of the grassy knoll to look at the water. Here, the stream was fairly wide and strewn with rocks. The water bubbled white as it tumbled over and rushed past the glistening rocks. The white feathers in the water glowed brightly in the moonlight while the water itself winked blackly, and the result was an exceptionally vivid contrast that made the stream even more beautiful at night than it was by day.

Marline felt drawn to the water, and she walked all the way down the knoll until she found a soft, wide spot in the grass. She sat down and pulled her knees up under her chin as she looked out at the water. Then she was struck with the overwhelming urge to take a bath.

And why not? It had been days since she had been able to take anything more than a sponge bath.

Marline walked back to her horse and dug through the saddlebag until she found a bar of soap. Although this soap, like the laundry soap, had been made by her mother, it had been sweetened by the addition of a few drops of perfume.

It was the middle of the night, and she was in the middle of nowhere, so she was certain there was no one around to see her. Stripping out of her clothes, she walked naked out into the water, carrying the perfumed bar of soap with her. She began splashing the water on her skin, luxuriating in the wonderful feeling of cleanliness. She was cognizant only of the delightful feeling of the water and the soap, and she paid absolutely no attention to the picture she might be presenting, since she was alone.

When Dick saw the horse he thought for a minute that it might be Ron Sietz. Then he realized that it couldn't be Ron. He and Ron were riding nighthawk, with Ron on the west side of the herd and Dick on the east. This horse was even farther to the east.

The horse was saddled and tethered. Dick didn't know who it belonged to, but he knew it didn't belong to anyone in his outfit.

Remembering the raid on his herd back at Trailback, when Moses and Danny were killed, Dick's senses were keen to danger. He dismounted, tied off his own horse, then pulled his pistol. Moving at a crouch and in as quick a loping gait as his game leg would allow, Dick maneuvered along the bottom of the knoll. When he saw the horse begin jerking its head and sniffing at the wind he stopped, fearing that if he got any closer to the animal it might give him away.

Dick climbed to the top of the knoll, then slipped down on the other side. He advanced along the edge of the stream, ready for whatever was ahead. Suddenly he stopped and stared in disbelief. There, clearly visible in the bright splash of moonlight, was Marline Konda.

What in the world was she doing here? Then he answered his own question. Obviously she was taking a bath, for she was standing in the water, lathered with soap and at the moment, stark naked. But why was she here, more than one hundred miles north of her ranch?

Even as he was wondering about such things, his perception of her was changed forever. No longer the little girl who had so often been in the way of his and Charley's play, what he was seeing now was a vision of pure loveliness. This was no little girl, this was a beautiful young woman with long, lean limbs, high-lifted breasts, and small, pink nipples.

Dick stood there for a long moment, mesmerized by the scene. Then, realizing that his undetected observation was a vulgar invasion of her privacy, he turned his back toward the water.

"Marline, what are you doing here?" he called out to her.

"What?" Marline shouted, shocked at being discovered. She spun around toward the sound of the voice, making a vain attempt to cover herself as she did so. She saw a man standing on the bank of the stream and, though she couldn't make out his features because he was standing in shadows, she had recognized his voice. "Dick, you should have made your presence known," she said harshly.

"I did," Dick replied. "I said, 'Marline, what are you doing here?'"

"Yes, I guess you did at that, didn't you?"

Dick could hear the ripple of water from behind him as Marline walked out of the stream. "Would you mind keeping your back to me until I am dressed?" she asked. "Although I suppose it's too late now."

"No, uh, I haven't seen anything," Dick said. It was a lie, but it was a lie he felt comfortable with because he didn't want to embarrass her anymore than he was sure he already had.

To Dick's surprise, Marline gave out a low, throaty laugh.

"Liar," she said easily. "If you didn't see

123

anything, how did you know it was me?"

"Uh, well, I turned around as soon as I realized," Dick said.

"You can turn around now."

Dick turned back just as Marline was packing her shirttail into her pants. Not fully buttoned, the shirt gapped open, and he could see droplets of water glistening on the globes of her breasts. He looked away in embarrassment as she finished the buttoning.

"What are you doing here?" Dick asked again.

"I came looking for you."

"You're looking for me? Why?"

"You know why."

Dick sighed. "Marline, you're going to ask me again if you can join my outfit, aren't you? Well, the answer was no when you asked the first time, and it's still no. Besides, I have three other men with me. One woman with four men simply wouldn't . . ."

"I have three other women with me," Marline said, interrupting Dick's protest.

"What?"

"And a thousand head of cattle."

"My God, Marline, what is this? What are you doing?"

"Your family isn't the only one that needs money," Marline said. "Nearly every ranch in the panhandle is in the same situation, including the Votaws, Driscolls, Blackburns, and my own folks. So I figured that what's sauce for the goose is sauce for the gander. If you can take your cows to the Dakota Territory, then so can we."

"So that was your plan? To join up with us so far away that we wouldn't send you back?" Dick asked.

"Yes," Marline admitted.

"What if it doesn't work? What if I said that you made it out here on your own, you can make it back?"

"We're not going back," Marline said.

"You aren't going back?"

"No. I would like an invitation to join you, Dick Hodson. And if you weren't so obstinate about it, you would realize that since there are four of you, and four of us, there would be more hands to ease the work load. But if you don't want us to join you, that's fine. Like I said, we're not going back. We'll just trail along behind, and all of us will work twice as hard as need be to get the herd to Dakota."

Frustrated by the turn of events, Dick ran his hand through his hair. "All right, you can join your herd to ours. But dammit, Marline, you are as big a pest as you ever were. You haven't changed one little bit," he said angrily.

"Why, Dick Hodson," Marline teased. "Do you mean to tell me after the eyeful you got a few minutes ago, that you can stand there and say I haven't changed one little bit?"

CHAPTER TEN

Windom, Texas

Joel Konda stopped the buckboard in front of the Texas Land Development Company office, set the brake, then hopped down. He tied the horses off at the hitching rail before he came back to the buckboard to help Trudy down.

Bryan Phelps stepped out onto the front porch of his office, smiling broadly.

"Mr. and Mrs. Konda, how nice of you to come," he greeted them enthusiastically. "Please, come inside. Have some champagne. I hope you don't mind, but I think this is a cause for celebration."

"What is there to celebrate?" Joel asked.

"Well for me, it's the acquisition of a good piece of property. And since I am paying handsomely for the property, you should celebrate the profit you are making."

"You think I am making a profit?"

"As I understand it, Mr. Konda, you inherited your ranch from your father. And as he was one of Texas' original homesteaders, he didn't actually pay anything for the land when he occupied it. Therefore anything you get from me could be considered one hundred percent profit."

"Mr. Phelps, my father fought with Sam Houston in Texas' War of Independence. I fought with Zachary Taylor in the Mexican War, and my son was killed fighting with Sterling Price in the War Between the States. Don't try and tell me that this land wasn't paid for. We have paid dearly."

Phelps cleared his throat. "Yes, well, I didn't mean that as it sounded. Of course you have an investment in the land. I was just calling to your attention the fact that I could wait and pick it up for taxes, in which case you would get nothing. Instead, I am paying you a fair price for your property. But enough of this, come on inside, both of you, please."

Phelps held the door open as first Trudy then Joel Konda filed into his office. On a table over to one side of the office sat a bottle of champagne and a tray of small pastries.

Phelps poured two glasses of champagne, then offered them to Joel and Trudy. "Here, have yourselves some champagne while I get the contract," he said. "Sit there at the table and make yourself comfortable. I'll only be a minute."

Joel and Trudy sat in the chairs Phelps had pointed out. Joel picked up the glass and looked at the sparkling wine. Sniffing it, he wrinkled his nose as it was tickled by the escaping bubbles and he quickly pulled the glass away. He slowly raised it to his lips and tasted it, then held it out and looked at it again.

"Something wrong?" Phelps asked as he rifled through papers on his desk.

"No," Joel said. "It's just that I ain't ever drunk champagne."

"Well, you should get used to it, Mr. Konda. As soon as we close our deal, you'll have enough money to retire and drink as much champagne as you ever want."

"I reckon I've already had all the champagne I ever want," Joel said, setting the still-filled glass down. Looking over at Trudy, Joel saw that she hadn't even picked up her glass.

"Ahh, here is the contract," Phelps said. "And as you can see, it is accompanied by a bank draft for fifteen thousand dollars." Phelps lay the contract and the bank draft on the table in front of Joel. Then he put an inkwell and pen before him. "I'll need you to sign right here," he said.

Joel picked up the contract, then began tearing it into strips.

"Here, what are you doing?" Phelps sputtered, shocked by Joel's action.

"I won't be signing any contract," Joel said. "And I won't be selling you my land."

"What? But I thought everything was all set. Mrs. Konda, will you talk some sense to your husband?" Phelps demanded.

Trudy took Joel's hand. "My husband *is* making sense," she said.

"You mean you go along with this?"

"Wholeheartedly."

"But we had a deal."

"No, sir, Mr. Phelps, we didn't have a deal. What we had was an offer. You figured you had us over a barrel and, for a while, I guess I thought you did, too. But there is no deal until the contract is signed, and I'm not signing."

"You're a fool."

"Could be."

Phelps stood there for a moment, in frustrated silence, then he made a wave with his hand. "I don't understand," he said. "If you knew you weren't going to sign the contract, why did you even bother to come in here today?"

"I don't know," Joel admitted. "I guess so I could tell you, man to man, that I don't want to sell you my land. Or it might have been because I just wanted to see my name on a bank draft that large."

As if suddenly remembering that the bank draft had been written, Phelps picked it up quickly and began tearing it up.

"Well, I hope, you got a good look at it, Konda," Phelps spat. "Because looking at it was as close to that much money as you'll ever get in your life."

"I'm sorry if we made you angry."

"Angry?" Phelps flashed a smile, though it was obviously without mirth. "Why should I be angry? I was just trying to be nice to you. Now I'll wait until the taxes are due. Then I'll pick up your ranch, and the ranches of every other penniless piece of Rebel trash." He pointed to the map on the wall, replete with all the cross-hatched property. "Within a year, I'll own the entire county."

"That's a possibility," Joel admitted. "But until that happens, the Tilted K is still mine. Come, Trudy, let's go home."

Clinging to her husband's arm, Trudy started out. Her eyes were glistening with tears of pride and determination.

"Konda," Phelps called to him, just before he reached the door. "What made you change your mind?"

"Not what, who," Joel answered. "My daughter made me change my mind."

"And how did she do that?"

"By having the courage I didn't have," Joel said. "She is taking some cows to market."

"What market? You know as well as I do there is no market around here."

"Yeah," Joel said, a sly smile playing across his face. "I know."

Phelps watched Joel and Trudy Konda climb into the buckboard and drive away.

Down the street from the office of the Texas Land Development Company was the Tumbleweed Saloon. Upstairs in her room over the saloon, Cassie Thomas sat at her dresser, trying with makeup to get rid of the puffiness around her red eyes. She had been crying because she had just learned from Dane Coleman that, despite her belief to the contrary, he had no intention of ever marrying her.

"I don't see why you are crying," Dane Coleman said when he saw her tears begin to flow.

"I'm crying because you lied to me. You told me you wanted to marry me. And now you say that isn't so."

Coleman laughed out loud. "Now, come on, Cassie. You are a whore, for crying out loud. You didn't actually think I meant what I said, did you? Nobody wants to marry a whore."

"I've known girls who were on the line who have gotten married," Cassie said. "It's the dream of every soiled dove."

"I wouldn't marry you if you were the last woman in Texas," Coleman said. He laughed again, a mirthless, derisive snarl of a laugh. "You must be crazy."

"Then why?"

"Why won't I marry you? Do I have to tell you why? I should think that would be obvious."

"No. I mean, why did you tell me you wanted to marry me?"

Now the snarling laugh turned to a chuckle of conquest. "It's a little trick I learned a long time ago, girlie," he said. "Tell a whore you want to marry them, and nine times out of ten they'll give you ever'thing they got for free. So that's what I done, and you fell for it, Cassie. Hook, line, and sinker."

With a little cry of hurt and anger, Cassie picked up the water pitcher from her dresser and hurled it toward Coleman. She missed him, but the vase shattered against the wall

133

behind the bed, showering Coleman with water. Little shards of glass made pin-pricks in his bald head, and when he reached his hand up, it came away with blood.

"Watch that, you dumb bitch! I could've been cut bad by that."

A loud knock at the door interrupted them.

"Who is it?" Coleman called out sharply.

"It's me — Phelps. Open the door."

"Wait," Cassie said, holding out her hand. "I'm naked. Let me get something on."

"You trying to tell me Phelps has never seen you naked?" Coleman asked as he opened the door.

As quickly as she could, Cassie covered herself with a shawl.

"Coleman, we've got problems," Phelps said, pushing into the room. He saw little streaks of blood streaming down from the top of Coleman's bald head. "What the hell happened to you?" If Phelps saw Cassie, he didn't even acknowledge her.

"Nothing, just a few scratches is all," Coleman said as he wiped the top of his head. "What's wrong?"

"It's Joel Konda. He just came by the office to back out of the deal. He says he isn't going to sell his land."

"That's not really a problem, is it, boss?"

Coleman asked. "I mean, like you said, you'll just pick up the property next year come tax time. His, and anybody else's that you want."

"Maybe not."

"What do you mean?"

"The Tilting K is like the Trailback, it's still pretty strong. All Konda needs is a little bit of cash to get him through."

Coleman smiled. "Well, there you go, boss. Where's he going to get the cash?"

"He told me that his daughter is driving some cattle to market up north."

"You mean she's joined with Hodson?"

Phelps shook his head. "I don't know whether she did or not. He didn't say. All he said is she is driving their herd up north. And I take it there are some others who went with her. It doesn't matter whether they have joined their herds or not. What does matter is if they find the market they are looking for, then everyone else will be doing the same thing. That could change everything around here."

"You think they'll find one?"

"They won't find a market in Texas, that's for sure. I've already made certain of that. But they might find one out of state, so the solution is to make sure that they don't get their herd to wherever it is they are headed.

135

In the meantime, I'll get a law passed making it illegal to transport a herd beyond the state lines."

"How are you going to do that?"

"By bribery," Phelps said easily. "I'm going to buy the position of administrator for the Federal Commission of Agriculture and Livestock overseeing the occupied State of Texas. My first act will be to prevent any Texas cattle from being sold to an out-of-state market, without commission approval."

"It's too late for that, isn't it?" Coleman asked. "I mean you have to figure that Hodson and Konda and the others have already left Texas with a herd."

"You forget, my commission will be federal, not state. My jurisdiction will reach across state lines."

"You aren't a federal administrator yet."

"I will be by the time you find that herd. Find them, and make certain they don't get to where they are going."

"How do you want me to stop them?"

"I don't care how you do it. Just do it."

After Dane Coleman and Bryan Phelps left the Tumbleweed Saloon, Cassie walked over to the window of her room and looked out onto the street. Dane Coleman was right about her. She had fallen for his deception. For the last six weeks she had allowed him access to her room — and to her body — anytime he wanted. And she hadn't charged him a cent for the privilege.

She did that because she didn't feel that it was right to charge the man you are going to marry. Also, because she didn't think she should continue to see other men during her engagement, she stopped inviting other customers up to her room. She gave up being a whore, and for several weeks tried to support herself just on the kickback she got from the drinks she sold. But that wasn't enough and, gradually, her small amount of savings began to disappear.

Cassie had not always been a soiled dove. Before the war started she had lived on a small ranch with her mother and father. But her father was killed during the war, and her mother died of the fever shortly thereafter. Cassie suddenly found herself at the tender age of fifteen with no means of support and no one to turn to. Out of a sense of desperation, she fell in to what other girls like her referred to as "the life."

Now it was time for her to leave the life. She realized that if she did this, she was going to have to go somewhere else. She would be unable to live an ordinary existence here, because too many people knew about her. But if she could leave Hutchinson County, if she could go north, she might be able to find another town, and some honest means of making a living. Without the stain of prostitution hanging over her, she might even find a young, single rancher somewhere, who would be willing to share his life with her.

Yes, she thought. That would be perfect. She certainly understood ranching, and she missed it desperately. She would make a good wife for some rancher just getting started. And if she was far enough away from any chance of being exposed, her new husband would never have to know about her unsavory background.

CHAPTER ELEVEN

On the Trail

The first gray light of morning broke upon two herds joined together as one. The sun, which was still low in the east, sent long bars of light slashing through the tall fir trees, and the morning mist curled around the tops of the trees like ghosts.

The three thousand head of cattle, now milling about on the plateau, represented the combined herds of eight different ranches. This was a critical time because the cows of the Hodson herd, representing four different ranches, had just gotten used to each other. Likewise the cows of the Konda herd, also representing four different ranches, had just gotten used to being together. Because the two herds were now mingled, the animals were acutely aware of different smells, sensations, and strangers in their midst. They would have to acclimate themselves all over again. This made them very nervous, and Dick knew that the least little thing could spook them: a wolf, a lightning flash, or a loud noise.

He listened with an analytical ear to the bawling of cattle. He was also aware of the shouts and whistles of the wranglers, male and female, and he realized that just as delicate as the co-mingling of the herds was the throwing together of riders.

For now, at least, everyone's mind was on the business at hand, which was making the joining of the two outfits as uneventful as possible. But later, when the cattle were once again calmed down and the long process of driving the herd north continued, would there be trouble? What if two of the men liked the same woman? Would there be jealousy? A fight?

Wait a minute, he thought. Forget about the others. What if someone else decides that he likes Marline?

Even as the thought came to him, he knew the answer. He wouldn't want anyone else to exhibit any interest in Marline. Looking toward Marline, he saw that she was totally unaware that she was the subject of his recent ruminations. Instead, Marline was concentrating on driving the herd. Dick watched her dash forward to intercept three or four steers who had moved away from the herd. She stopped the stragglers and pushed them back with the others. Dick couldn't help but marvel at how well Marline could ride. It was almost as if she and the horse were sharing the same musculature and brain.

The women had come this far without a wagon, depending on their saddlebags as a means of supplying everything they needed, including food. On the other hand, the men had the wagon that Dick and his father had assembled from bits and pieces of other wagons. The vehicle was being drawn by a particularly fine-looking team of mules, and it was serving them well. The only problem was, no one really wanted to drive the wagon. Therefore, in order to be fair, they had drawn up a schedule, dividing up the detail equally. Everyone took their turn at the odious task, including Dick. On the day he was selected to drive, he would have to detach himself from the drive and go on ahead, stopping first for the noonday meal, then pushing on ahead even farther at a faster rate. That way he could have camp established and supper cooked by the time the weary cowboys were ready to eat.

Once the two herds joined, however, that all changed. To the joy of everyone concerned, Kitty Blackburn volunteered to drive the chuck wagon and become the permanent cook. From a purely practical point of view, her volunteering was the perfect match of ability and opportunity. Kitty was the least skilled in all the other aspects of the drive. She didn't ride very well, she couldn't work with rope, she was not a good shot, and though she wouldn't admit it to anyone, she was actually frightened of cows.

On the other hand, even the other women agreed that Kitty was the best cook of them all. That unique set of circumstances was the catalyst that allowed the two groups to come together harmoniously.

Whereas the men had brought nothing in the way of foodstuff but the barest necessities, the women augmented their fare with dried fruits and various herbs and spices. Those additions caused the food on the drive to improve from barely edible to more than tolerable. Kitty earned her place in the hearts of everyone the very first morning when she made flapjacks for breakfast.

Sometime after breakfast, with the herd now on the move, Dick rode back to their overnight camp to check on how Kitty was getting along. With the breakfast dishes clean, she was readying the chuck wagon for the day's run.

"Are you finding everything that you need?" Dick asked. Dick walked over to the side and tied a knot in a hanging piece of rawhide cord. Each knot represented a day, while a double-knot indicated a Sunday. As he knew what day they left, the strip of rawhide served as an effective calendar.

"Yes," Kitty replied. "I must say, whoever laid out this wagon did an excellent job."

"Thanks," Dick said.

"You did it?"

"My pa and I did." Dick ran his hand lightly across the chuck-box, which was a shelf of honeycombs and cubbyholes. "I've always rather liked chuck wagons."

"I can tell. It's obvious this was a labor of love," Kitty said as she rubbed down the cutting board.

One of Dick's earliest memories was of hanging around the chuck wagon during roundups at Trailback. He could remember how fascinated he was by the construction of the chuck box. The chuck box sat at the rear of the wagon, with a hinged lid which let down onto a swinging leg to form a worktable. Here, the cook stored his utensils and whatever food he might use during the day; such things as flour, sugar, dried fruit, coffee beans, pinto beans, tobacco, "medicinal" whiskey, and, on occasion, hard candy.

What Kitty didn't know was that Dick didn't just design this chuck wagon. During the war it had become his totem, and he had built it in his mind several times over. It was the means he used to take away the boredom of long, stupefying encampments. It was a method of fighting fear on those terrifying nights before a battle. Later, when he was a prisoner of war, he made several mental refinements to the chuck wagon in order to survive the brutal conditions of the prison. This wagon represented the end result of all those months of planning. It was a personal triumph of proportions that no one else could possibly understand.

"I want you to know that we all appreciate your volunteering to take this job," Dick said after he tied the knot in the cord. "And if you need anything, let me know."

"Believe me, I'd much rather be doing this than messing around with cows," Kitty replied. "I know I don't sound much like a rancher's daughter, but I really don't like the foul beasts." She nodded toward the coffee pot which was still suspended over the open fire. "Would you like a cup of coffee before I pour the last of it out and get underway?"

"Yes, thank you, that would be nice," Dick said.

Kitty reached for a cup, but put it back when she saw Dick take a folding cup from his saddlebag. Using a pad of towels as a shield against the heat of the handle, she removed the coffee pot from the fire. "How far do you think I should go before I stop to fix lunch?" she asked as she poured coffee.

"Oh, I figure we'll be about ten miles on at lunchtime. You should beat us there very easily. You'll have plenty of time to stop, start your fire, make the coffee, and have something ready for us. We eat light at lunch, maybe no more than a biscuit and a piece of bacon, or a cup of soup . . . something like that. As soon as you can after lunch, you'll need to go on ahead until you reach a good place for our night camp. Our suppers are generally a lot bigger than the lunch."

"All right," Kitty said. "Oh, and Mr. Hodson," she started.

"It's Dick," Dick interrupted. "I admit that I've taken on the responsibility of leading the drive, but I don't really think of myself as a trail boss. The way I look at it, we've all got cows invested so that sort of makes us all equal in this outfit."

"All right, then, Dick," Kitty corrected. "I want to thank you for letting us join you. We discussed it quite a bit while we were on the way here. We weren't sure you would welcome us."

Dick chuckled. "Well, the truth is I wouldn't have, but you sort of forced the issue on us," Dick said. "Showing up out here the way you did didn't leave us much of a choice but to accept you."

"I know," Kitty replied. "That was the way we had it planned. At least, that's the way Marline had it planned. This was all her idea."

"I thought as much."

"Wait a minute, don't get me wrong, I'm not blaming Marline, I'm giving her credit for coming up with the idea," Kitty said. "I think driving a herd from Texas to Dakota is the most splendid thing I have ever heard of, not only for the money it will bring our families, but because it is a wonderful adventure."

Dick chuckled. "I'll give you that. It is an adventure, all right."

In the distance, Dick could see Priscilla and Ron working to keep the herd moving in the right direction. Though the two outfits had only been together for a few hours, there was already an economy of effort between them, and the men and women rode together as if they had been doing it for a long time.

"I have to admit that I was against it when she first proposed the idea," Dick said. "But I'm beginning to think I may have been wrong. This might work out very well as long as we don't have any, uh . . ." he paused in midsentence.

"Any boyfriend-girlfriend trouble, you mean?" Kitty asked.

Dick nodded. "Something like that, yes."

"Don't you think we can be trusted?"

"It's not that. It's just that, well, we have a long drive ahead of us. And we are going to be spending a lot of time together. Under such conditions, things seem to have a way of getting difficult."

"It will only get difficult if we let it get difficult," Kitty said.

Dick smiled. "You're a smart girl, Kitty."

Kitty chuckled. "Yes, that's what they always say about me. 'That's Kitty Blackburn, Caleb and Roberta's daughter,'" Kitty said, imitating one of the town's people. "'She's a smart 'un, all right. Make's a fine schoolmarm.'"

Dick laughed at Kitty's imitation.

"I'm sure they will all be shocked when they learn that I have embarked upon such an adventure as this."

"You know who wouldn't have been shocked?" Dick said. "Your brothers, Travis and Troy. Not only would they not be shocked, they would be proud of you."

Kitty's twin brothers had both been killed in the war.

"I like to think that," Kitty said. She smiled, sadly. "But of course, if they were still here, they would have been on this drive instead of me."

"And I would love to have had them with me," Dick replied. He drained the rest of his coffee, then collapsed his cup and put it back in his saddlebag. "But I have to say that if I can't have them, having their sister is the next best thing." Dick swung back into his saddle. "I'll see you at lunch," he said.

Kitty watched Dick ride back out toward the herd, then turned her attention to the task at hand, making the chuck wagon ready for the day's transit.

Although Cassie Thomas had made her living as a whore for the last three years, she was, and always had been, a very good horsewoman. By riding hard for two days, she overtook the cattle drive and found herself riding toward the camp about suppertime.

"Hello the camp!" she called as she approached, materializing out of the darkening gloom.

"Who's that?" Buck asked.

"There's only one rider," Dooley said.

"Sounded like a woman," Marline suggested.

Buck stood up. "One rider that we can see," he said, taking a drink of coffee and staring out toward the lone, approaching rider.

"Well, I'll be damned!" Ron suddenly said. "Uh, excuse my language, ladies," he apologized quickly.

"Never mind that. What is it?" Marline asked with obvious curiosity in her voice.

Ron pointed toward the rider. "That's Cassie Thomas."

"Cassie Thomas? What's she doing out here?" Priscilla asked.

"Hello the camp!" Cassie called again, stopping now, and waiting until she was invited to proceed farther.

"Come on in," Dick called back to her.

"Thanks."

"Who is Cassie Thomas?" Buck asked.

"She's a whore," Dooley answered. Dooley's answer was neither accusatory nor condemning. It was merely a statement of fact.

"I hope she isn't out here trying to drum up a little business," Kitty said with a nervous laugh. "Because if she is, it could get a little awkward."

149

Dick chuckled. "I doubt that it is anything like that," he said.

Cassie came all the way into camp, then dismounted.

"Thanks for the invite," she said as she wrapped the reins of her horse around a small shrub.

"We've got a little supper left," Marline said. "You're welcome to it."

"Thanks," Cassie replied. "I'll take you up on that kind offer. I've had nothing but jerky for a couple of days now."

"Kitty, will you rustle something up for her?" Dick asked, and Kitty quickly began spooning beans, bacon, and rice into a pan. A moment later, Cassie was sitting on a log eating the meal with gusto. "Coffee?" Kitty offered.

"Yes, thanks."

"Miss Thomas," Dick started, and Cassie laughed so hard that she spit out a mouthful of beans.

"What is it?" Dick asked. "Did I say something funny?"

Cassie put her hand over her mouth to control her laughter, and she shook her head. Finally settling, she looked at Dick with eyes still full of humor.

"I'm sorry," she said. "It's just that you called me Miss Thomas, and I don't think

I've ever been called that in my entire life."

"What should I call you?"

"You could call me Cassie," she said. Then she paused, as if contemplating something momentous. "No, better yet, why don't you call me Opal?"

"Opal?"

"Opal is my real name. I took up the name Cassie Thomas when I went into the life. Lots of girls who are on the line do that. We don't want to shame our family name none. I had no family left to shame, but I didn't want to stain the Foster name."

"Foster?" Dick asked with piqued interest. "Your name is Foster?"

"Opal Foster."

"Look here, your father wouldn't be Marlon Foster, would he? Colonel Marlon Foster?"

"Yes, that was my father. Did you know him?"

"Everyone who survived Shiloh knew him, for we all owe our lives to him," Dick said. "On the day General Beauregard retired from the field, your father's regiment held Grant's army back for nearly eight hours. Of the six hundred and thirty-two men of your father's regiment who were committed to the fight, but forty-one survived. Colonel Foster was one of those who died, but not until he had seen his regiment make our withdrawal possible. Had he not done so, we would have lost thousands more including, perhaps, me."

"I knew it," Opal said, her eyes shining brightly. "I was never able to get word as to how my father died, because after I changed my name, no one knew how to find me. But, somehow, I knew my father had died heroically."

"No man ever died more bravely, nor by his death, saved more men."

"Thank you for sharing that with me," Opal said.

"I'm honored to be able to get some recognition for that gentleman where it is truly deserved, within his own family. But I'm curious, Opal, what brings you out here?"

Opal thought about the scene she had experienced with Dane Coleman, and the process she had gone through in making the decision to leave Windom. She didn't want to share with her new friends the humiliation she had suffered at Coleman's hands.

"I've decided to give up whorin'," Opal said.

"Good for you," Priscilla responded heartily.

"I know it is something I should have

done long ago, but whorin' is all I've known since I was fifteen."

"Fifteen?" Kitty gasped. "You've been, uh, doing this since you were fifteen?"

"Looked to me like I had no choice. My pa was killed early in the war, and my ma died right after that. I had no one to turn to, and no way of making a living. Whorin' was the only way I could support myself," Opal said.

"That's awful," Marline said with compassion.

"Believe me, my story isn't unique," Opal said. "Half the whores I've ever known didn't set out to get into the life."

"If whoring is all you have ever known, what do you plan to do now?" Marline asked.

Opal shook her head. "I really don't know the answer to that question," she said. "All I am sure of is that I don't want to whore anymore. But since everyone back in Hutchinson County knows me, and knows what I did for a living, whatever I wind up doing will have to be done somewhere else."

"Probably not a bad idea," Dick agreed.

Over the rim of her coffee cup, Opal studied both Dick and Marline. "So, you've put the two herds together. Phelps and Coleman were wondering if you were going to join the two, or take two separate herds up to Dakota."

"I beg your pardon?" Dick asked in surprise. "Phelps and Coleman were discussing our business?"

"They were discussing it, and are probably still discussing it," Opal said. "I know you didn't ask for my advice, but if you were to ask, I would tell you to be very careful."

"Why is that?" Marline asked.

"Because Dane Coleman is coming after you," Opal said matter-of-factly.

"How do you know?" Dick asked.

"I overheard Coleman and Phelps talking," Opal explained. "Phelps is upset because you are making this drive."

"I don't understand," Marline said. "Why would it matter to them whether or not we take our cows to Dakota?"

"Well, for one thing, wasn't your pa going to sell his ranch to Phelps?"

"What? Yes. Wait a minute, what do you mean *was* he going to sell?"

"He took back his offer. He isn't going to sell his ranch, now."

"He isn't?" Marline asked, gleefully. "That's wonderful news. But I don't understand. What made him change his mind?"

Opal chuckled. "You did, by making this drive."

"How did he even know about this drive? I didn't tell him I was making it. I didn't tell anyone. I just left," Marline replied.

"I don't know how he knew, but he knew. And he told Phelps that he wasn't going to sell his ranch now."

"Huzzah!" Marline said, clapping her hands together. "I was hoping Pa would have second thoughts."

"He did. And now Phelps is afraid a lot of other people are going to have second thoughts, too. Especially if you make it. You'd be surprised at how many people back in the panhandle are pulling for you to be successful."

"I'll bet," Dooley said.

"Of course, there are also those who don't want you to make it, including Phelps. He is afraid if you get through with your cows, others will be encouraged to try the same thing. And if that happens, he is going to lose a great deal of money."

"Ha. That's just too bad," Ron said.

"Could be. But like I said, Dane Coleman is coming after you."

"What does he plan to do when he catches up to us?" Dick asked.

"I don't know," Opal answered. "And I don't believe Coleman knows, either. But Phelps told him to stop you by whatever means it takes, so Coleman will do it. Or at least, he will try to do it. And believe me, Coleman can be cruelly inventive."

Chapter Twelve

Opal spent the night with them by invitation, and, as they sat around the breakfast fire the next morning, she was asked if she would like to join the outfit.

"You don't want me," Opal protested.

"If you had come here a couple of weeks ago, I would agree with you," Dick replied. "Before we left Texas, Marline asked if she could come with me, and I said no. It was nothing against her, I just didn't want any women with us. Then when Marline and the other women suddenly showed up, I let them join us because I didn't think I had any choice. But now that they have joined us, it's hard to imagine making this drive without them. They're pulling their weight, just like the men, and believe me, we can use every rider we can get."

"You don't understand, I'm not just an ordinary woman. I'm a whore."

"Oh? I thought you told us yesterday that

you had quit that," Marline said.

"I have, and I don't intend to ever do it again," Opal replied. "But until I prove myself, people will still call me a whore."

Dick laughed. "They won't call you a whore around Ron Sietz," he said. "That is, not if they want to keep all their teeth."

The others, who by now had heard the story of how Ron whipped the Yankee soldier for calling Cassie a whore, laughed as well.

Opal looked at Ron in surprise. "You mean what they were saying back in town is true? You really did fight someone because he called me a whore?"

"Yes'm," Ron said, looking at the ground in embarrassment.

Opal smiled at Ron. "I don't know what to say, except that no woman has ever been more flattered, nor less deserving, to have someone come to her defense."

"Well, the truth is, ma'am, that Yankee was a surly son of a bitch, and I was just looking for some reason to whup him," Ron said. At that pronouncement everyone, including Opal, laughed.

"Opal, everyone is entitled to a new beginning," Kitty said. "I won't presume to speak for the others, but for my part, you are more than welcome to join us."

"That goes for me, too," Anita said.

"And me," Priscilla put in.

Opal turned and walked away from the others.

"What's wrong, Opal?" Dick called. "Did we make you angry?"

"Dick, you might be doing a good job running this outfit," Marline said. "But you don't know much about women, do you?"

"What do you mean?"

"Give someone a little privacy when they want to cry."

"Cry? What's she crying about?"

"Nothing," Opal said, turning back toward them as she wiped the tears from her eyes. "I'd be very happy to join the outfit."

The little group of men and women drovers crossed the Indian Territory's Cimarron Strip without incident, then moved up into southwestern Kansas. As each day passed the wranglers grew more comfortable with the trail experience, and they established a rhythm that enabled them to work exceptionally well together, each drawing upon the strength of the others.

Each passing day also brought with it a sense of relief that Coleman hadn't tried anything to interrupt the drive. For the first few days after Opal's warning, they were constantly looking over their shoulders, absolutely positive that Coleman would show up at any moment.

When he didn't materialize, they began to harbor first the hope, and then the belief, that perhaps they had come too far away for Phelps to pursue them. Everyone but Dick quit worrying about him.

Dick might have been harboring some lingering worry about Dane Coleman, but he was no longer fretting about any troubles stemming from the result of throwing young men and young women together in such close proximity. He feared that romances might develop, but that concern seemed unfounded. The young men and women did tend to team up with each other, but the pairing off seem more of a working alliance than any sort of romantic connection.

As usual, the entire outfit ate breakfast together; those who had been riding since midnight, and those who had just been awakened to start the new day. While they were having their breakfast, Dick noticed that Anita seemed a little detached. While the others talked, she walked around, pulling stems of grass and sucking on the roots, snapping twigs and smelling them, and scooping up a handful of dirt to examine it very closely.

Finally Dick's curiosity got the best of him.

"Anita, you want to tell me what you are looking for?" he asked.

"What's the name of that river you say we'll be crossing next?"

"The Arkansas."

"How far do you make it from here?"

"I'd say another seventy to eighty miles."

"They're going to be dry miles," Anita said. "From the looks of the sign, there hasn't been a rain here in quite a spell. Like as not, any watering holes between here and the Arkansas are likely to be dried up."

"That's not good," Dick said. "We've got maybe three days to go."

"Any year-round streams or creeks that you know of between here and there?"

Dick shook his head. "There's nothing on the map, and I've never been up here myself, so I don't know."

"Dick, if it's going to be as dry as Anita says, the herd is going to get awfully thirsty," Marline warned. "And when cows get thirsty, they spook very easily."

"I know," Dick said. "Riders, be very careful when you are driving them. Don't make any sudden movements or noises. Something as ordinary as taking the saddle blanket off your horse could spook them into stampede."

"Any of you ever seen a stampede?" Kitty asked in a worried voice as she took a couple of extra pancakes out of the skillet for Ron.

"No, I haven't," Marline answered. "Have you, Dick?"

"I can't say as I have," Dick admitted. "That is, I've never seen a full-blown stampede of as many cows as we have here. But I have seen smaller herds panic and run, and believe me, I got out of the way even then. If this herd goes, we'll have our hands full, I can promise you that."

"What's the best thing to do if they start to stampede?" Buck asked.

"First thing you do is get the hell out of their way," Dick replied. "Ladies, excuse the language."

"Seems appropriate in a case like this," Priscilla said, and the others chuckled.

"The next thing, after you get out of the way, is just follow them, and when they run down a little so you can turn them, try and head them back in the right direction. But the best thing to do is keep them from stampeding in the first place."

Over the next two days the Hodson Outfit, as they were now calling themselves, moved as gingerly as if they were walking on thin ice. They made no sudden movements, whether mounted or not, and when they spoke to each other it was in whispers. Their caution was paying off, though, and as dawn broke on the third day, Dick began to believe that they were going to get through the dry spell without too much difficulty. Buck had ridden ahead the day before, and returned to tell them that they were only ten miles away from water.

Dane Coleman had been following the herd for three days, looking for some opportunity to stop them. As he had suspected, the Konda girl had joined her herd with Hodson's herd. He wasn't sure how he felt about that. On the one hand, having all the cows in one place had made the job of locating them easier. On the other hand, had the herds remained separate, it would have been easier to deal with them on an individual basis, especially the women.

Yesterday, Coleman had gotten close enough to see that one of the women was Cassie Thomas. He had been very surprised by that. He knew she had left town, but not in his wildest imagination would he have believed she would join these people.

The night Coleman left Windom, he had gone over to the Tumbleweed Saloon to apologize to Cassie. It wasn't that he actually thought he had something to apologize about, but he did have a good thing going as long as she believed he intended to marry her. And he wasn't ready to blow that off just yet.

When he started banging on the door to her room at the Tumbleweed, he was told that she had cashed in all her chits[*] and left town. It didn't really bother him that much. There were other soiled doves around. Besides, Cassie was getting to be a little too feisty for him, anyway.

Nevertheless, he was surprised to find her out here on the trail with Dick Hodson and his outfit, and he wondered what she was doing here. Then he remembered that she had been present when Phelps instructed him to stop the drive, no matter what it took.

Had Cassie turned against him? Had she come up here to warn them? No, he thought, answering his own question. She'd

---

*Prostitutes were often paid in copper coins, called "chits" redeemable at the saloon where the girls worked. The chits were so well valued that in some Western towns they were legal tender in other places of business as well. There are even some examples of chits turning up in the collection plates on Sunday.

probably just thrown in with them so she wouldn't have to ride by herself. Besides, even if Cassie had told them anything, what would make them believe her? Her reputation as a whore preceded her.

It didn't take long for Coleman to realize what Anita had pointed out to Dick. The trail was as dry as a bone, and conditions were ripe for a stampede. For a while, Coleman did nothing, hoping that nature would take its course, and the herd would stampede on its own. After all, the cows were hot, tired, thirsty, and becoming noticeably more restless with each passing moment.

But they were into the third day now, and Coleman knew that they had to be very close to water. Hodson and the others were working the perimeters expertly, moving the cows steadily and confidently. Despite their terrible thirst, the herd was well under control. On the third day, Coleman realized that if anything was going to happen, he was going to have to make it happen, and he was going to have to do it within the next couple of hours.

Getting into position where he was unseen by the drovers, Coleman pulled his pistol and fired a shot into the air.

Hearing the shot, Dick reacted at once.

"No! Who fired that shot?"

As Dick feared it would, the pistol shot frightened the cows into an immediate response. The cows nearest the shot started running, and that spread through the rest of the herd. Then, like a wild prairie fire before a wind, the herd was out of control. Exhilarated by his success, Coleman rode down toward the herd, firing several more shots to keep them going.

"Stampede! Stampede!" Buck shouted from the front, and his cry was carried in relay until everyone knew about it.

"Stampede!"

There was terror in the cry, and yet grim determination, too, for every man and woman who issued the cry moved quickly to do what they could to stop it.

Dick was riding on the left flank when the herd started running. Fortunately for him, the herd headed toward the right, a living tidal wave of thundering hooves, nearly a million aggregate pounds of muscle and bone, horn and hair, red eyes, dry tongues, and running noses. Three thousand animals were welded together as if they were one gigantic, raging beast.

A cloud of dust rose up from the herd and billowed high into the air. The air was so thick with dust that within moments Dick could see nothing. It was as if he were caught in the thickest fog one could imagine, but this fog was brown, and it burned the eyes and clogged the nostrils and stung his face with its fury. And it was filled with thousands of pounding hooves and slashing horns.

Dick managed to overtake the herd, then he rode to their right, trying desperately to turn them back into the proper direction. He, like the others, was shouting and whistling and waving his hat at the herd, trying to get them to respond. That was when he got a glimpse, just out of the corner of his eye, of Anita falling from her horse. The stampeding cows altered their rush just enough to come toward her, and she stood up and tried to outrun them, though it was clear that she was going to lose the race.

Dick acted without thinking. He headed right for Anita, even though it meant riding into the face of the stampede. When he came even with her, he reached down and picked her up with one arm, thankful that she was as small as she was. He hoisted the girl up under his arm and turned his horse to get away from the herd. As he reached the edge, the cows turned again, and Dick and Anita were safe. He set her back down, then rode off to join the others until they finally managed to bring the herd to a halt. The cows slowed from a mad dash to a brisk trot, and when they did, the wranglers were able to turn them back in the direction they were supposed to be going.

Within another hour the herd caught the scent of water as they approached the Arkansas River. They began moving toward the water at a quick gait that brought them to the water's edge within a few minutes.

The lead cows moved out into the river and for a moment, Dick was afraid that the cows coming up from behind would push the front ranks into deep water where they would drown. Fortunately, they had approached the river where a huge sandbar formed a natural ford, and the cattle were able to spread out enough so that all were able to drink their fill.

Although they had only come ten miles today, it had been an unusually rapid ten miles, so rapid that they had overtaken, then outpaced the chuck wagon. Dick called a halt to the drive, declaring that they would spend the next twenty-four hours camped right here.

An initial count of the herd turned up about two hundred missing cows, though by nightfall, all but eighty had found their way back to the herd and, more importantly, the water. All agreed that they had been very lucky they didn't lose any more animals than they had.

"Yeah, well, forget about the cows," Buck said. "We almost lost Anita. Would have, if it hadn't been for Dick."

Besides Buck, and of course Anita, several others had also seen the rescue. Dick's heroic action became the center of conversation around the campfire, and he was the subject of some gentle teasing.

"You do anything like that again and we'll have to get you a white horse and a set of shining armor," Dooley suggested, and the others laughed.

Ron walked over to the campfire and took out a burning brand to light his pipe. When he had it going, he sat down on a rock and puffed contentedly as he stared into the flames and the tiny red sparks that rode the heat waves up into the night sky, there to join with the stars.

"Well, we almost got to the river without 'em stampeding," Ron said. "If something hadn't set them off, we would have made it."

"It wasn't some*thing*, it was some*body*," Dick said. "Just before it started, I heard shots."

"Shots? Not one of us?" Ron asked.

"No, not one of us."

"Who, then? Did you see anyone?"

Dick shook his head. "No."

"It was Dane Coleman," Opal said.

"How do you know? Did you see him?" Kitty asked.

"I didn't have to see him. I know that's who it was."

"Doesn't seem likely he would come this far up," Buck suggested.

"You don't know Dane Coleman," Opal said.

"No, I don't. I take it you do know him?"

"I know him well," Opal said. "Though not as well as I once thought I did." She didn't elaborate, and the others didn't press further.

With the conversation stilled, the only sounds for several moments were the snap and pop of the fire, the whisper of the river, and the quiet grunts and the clacking of horns from the resting herd. During that time, Dick used the light of the camp fire to study the map.

"Uh-huh, it's just as I thought," he said after a while, almost as if he was talking to himself.

"What is what you thought?" Ron asked.

"The stampede moved us quite a way to the east of our original course," Dick said.

"That won't be a problem will it?" Dooley asked.

"No," Dick said. "In fact, it might work out even better. I had planned on bypassing the town of Mudflats. But since we are this close, we may as well go through it."

"Town?" Buck asked with a wide smile on his face. "We're goin' into a town? When?"

"Looks like we can get to it by tomorrow night," Dick replied. "I don't know how much of a town it is, though. According to the way they have it listed on the map it can't be very large."

"It doesn't make any difference," Dooley said. "A town is a town."

"Huzzah!" Ron yelled, and everyone joined him.

CHAPTER THIRTEEN

Mudflats, Kansas

Had Dick come into Mudflats, he would have seen that it was even smaller than he thought. It consisted of exactly four buildings; an outhouse, two warehouses, and a saloon. The outhouse was the only building made of lumber. The other three buildings were made of the mud bricks that gave the town its name.

Despite the modest size of the town, the saloon was surprisingly busy, filled as it was with nearly two dozen buffalo hunters who had chosen the town of Mudflats for a rendezvous. But one customer, standing at the end of the bar and staring morosely into his glass of whiskey, was not a buffalo hunter. Dane Coleman was somber because the stampede had failed to stop the drive.

Coleman had thought that starting a stampede would scatter cows from pillar to post, beyond any chance of Hodson ever recovering them. After all, the only people he had riding with him were a bunch of kids, and half of them were women. In fact, he had started back toward Windom when something told him to wait and make certain. So later that afternoon he rode back to see how it went, only to discover them camping idyllically along the side of the river.

All right, so the stampede didn't work. But he couldn't give up now — he would have to do something. He had no intention of going back to Bryan Phelps just to tell him that he had not been able to stop the cattle drive. Phelps wasn't the kind of person one could admit failure to.

"Mister, you goin' to drink that whiskey, or are you just plannin' on lookin' it outta that glass," someone asked gruffly.

Coleman looked up in quick anger. Then, when he saw the bewhiskered, scarred face of Emil Sawyer he smiled, broadly.

"Sawyer! You old horse thief! I thought for sure someone woulda shot you by now." The two men shook hands.

"Shh!" Sawyer said, putting his finger across his lips. "These here folks don't know I'm a horse thief. They think I'm a genuine war hero."

"Well, we are war heroes," Coleman said.

"We won the war, didn't we?"

"Hell, we was Jayhawkers," Sawyer said. "It didn't make any difference to us who won the war. You know and I know that whenever we looted and burned some Missouri farmer out, we didn't care whether he was loyal to the North or the South. We was doin' it for ourselves, not for the Union. Same as Quantrill's bunch was doin' it for themselves and not for the Confederacy."

"Yes, but we told folks we was fightin' for the Union, and the Union won," Coleman said. "That makes us heroes, while the ones who rode with Quantrill is outlaws."

Sawyer laughed. "You want to call me a hero, who am I to fight it?" He lifted his glass. "To us war heroes."

"To us," Coleman replied, taking a drink from his own glass. He wiped his mouth with the back of his hand. "So, what are you doing here in this godforsaken place. What's it called? Mudflats?"

"Some calls it that."

"Ain't much of a town," Coleman said.

"Hell, it ain't no town a'tall," Sawyer replied. "They wouldn't even have the place on the map except that it's a rendezvous for buffalo hunters. All there is to it is just this here saloon. Fella by the name of Ike Horner owns this saloon and the two warehouses outside. He trades with the Indians and the buffers, and anyone else that comes through. But don't nobody live here full-time."

Coleman looked around the saloon. In addition to the man tending bar, there were maybe twenty others.

"Is that what all these folks are doin' here?" Coleman asked. "They just passin' through?"

"They're here, same as me. They're buffin'," Sawyer replied.

"Buffin'?"

"Huntin' buffalo. We was told there was a herd seen down here, but that turned out to be a lie. I figure whoever found the actual herd sent us down here so's he could have more of it for hisself."

"Damn, Sawyer, what do you do with them hairy beasts when you find 'em?" Coleman asked.

"I butcher 'em and sell the meat to the railroad."

"What railroad?"

"Why, the Union Pacific Railroad," Sawyer said. "Where you been? The UP is layin' track all the way to California, didn't you know that?"

Coleman shook his head. "Nope. Hadn't heard anything about it."

"Well, they're doin' it all right. An' they got lots of workers to feed, so they're payin' six cents a pound for butchered buffalo meat."

"Six cents a pound doesn't sound like much. Especially if you have to trim him out."

"They ain't hard to trim out. We just take the easy, choice cuts. That comes to about five hunnert pounds including, of course, the pelt. We leave the rest. Pisses the Indians off, but there ain't nothin' they can do about it. We get thirty dollars for the meat and another six for the pelt."

Coleman stared at Sawyer as he drank his whiskey. "That's pretty good money," he said.

"Yeah," Sawyer agreed. He paused for a moment. "Well, it would be good money if there was any buffalo around. Thing is, it's too hot for 'em down here this time of year. I reckon by now they're all up north of the Republican."

"What about beef?" Coleman asked. "What would the railroad pay for beef?"

"I know what you're thinkin'," Sawyer said, "but the railroad has a fixed price. They pay six cents a pound, whether it's beef, buffalo, or chicken. That's the bad side. The good side is, buffalo you got to trim out, but they'll take beef on the hoof. The reason is that they can pen up the cows. That keeps the meat fresh on the hoof, so to speak. You can't keep buffalo in a pen."

"On the hoof, you say? So, a steer that weighs eight hunnert pounds would bring forty-eight dollars. Why, that's even better than a buff."

Sawyer shook his head. "They ain't none of 'em weighs that much."

"Sure there is. Some weighs even more than that."

"Not to the railroad they don't. You gotta remember, it's the people with the money who tell you how much the critters weigh, and in their book, ever' steer weighs five hunnert pounds. By the time you drive all the critters up here from Texas, why, it pure ain't worth it."

"What if I told you I knew where there was a herd of three thousand Texas Long-horns already up here, just waitin' to be took."

"Wild cows? Hell, they're as hard to keep penned up as buffalo."

Coleman signaled Horner to bring the bottle. As he spoke, he refilled Sawyer's glass. "These here ain't wild cows," he explained. "It's a herd that was put together with cows from eight ranches. It's bein' ramrodded by a fella by the name of Hodson. Do you know 'im?"

Sawyer shook his head. "No, should I? Who is he?"

"He was in the Texas Cavalry, I think. Got hisself wounded, then captured in one of them battles back East some'ers. Finally wound up in a prison camp up north, from what I hear. Still walks with a game leg."

"You met the fella?"

"Yeah, I met him. Fact is, the man I work for offered him a job."

"He must be a pretty good man if your boss tried to hire him."

"He's Rebel trash, like all the rest of them Texas bastards. What about it, Sawyer? You interested in takin' the herd away from him?"

"He ain't movin' the herd by hisself, is he? How many drovers has he got with him? Fifteen? Twenty? You might not remember, but we run up against some Texas Cavalry once. It was like bein' in a hornets' nest. Thankee just the same, but I ain't all that anxious to run into them fellers again."

"He's only got eight others with him," Coleman said. "And three of 'em is just kids, seventeen, maybe eighteen years old."

"Uh-huh," Sawyer said as he took another drink. "What I didn't tell you was that half them Texas cavalrymen wasn't no older'n that. Believe me, the bullets they shoot can kill you just as dead as bullets a thirty-year-old man shoots."

"All right, but now listen to this. Five of the ones he's got ridin' with him is women," Coleman added.

"Women drovers?" Sawyer asked in surprise.

"Well, four of the women is drovers. One of 'em is a whore," Coleman said.

Sawyer laughed. "A whore? On a cattle drive? You're not serious. What's a whore doing on a cattle drive?"

"She's tryin' to run away from bein' a whore, I reckon," Coleman answered. "The point is, I know the girl and she's a whore, through and through."

"How is it that you know so much about this herd?"

"I'm workin' with a fella who bought up a lot of Texas land after the war was over. The war was particularly hard on the folks down in the Panhandle. Seems like nearly every rancher down there lost a son or two. Because of that there wasn't a whole lot of fightin' spirit left in them. So when Colonel Phelps started buyin' up the place . . ."

"*Colonel* Phelps?" Sawyer interrupted.

"What kind of colonel? Confederate or Union?"

"Union," Coleman answered. "Hell, the only people down there with money now are former Union soldiers. Anyhow, when Phelps offered to buy their land for pennies on the dollar, most of 'em sold out to him."

"I thought Texans was supposed to be proud people. Who woulda thought they'd sell their land to an outsider like that?" Sawyer asked. "Especially a Union man."

"Most of 'em didn't have no choice. Right now, cows in Texas aren't worth what it costs to feed 'em. And Phelps aims to keep it that way. As long as cows are cheap, the ranchers can't make a livin', and that's the way he wants it."

"So, what's all that got to do with this herd you're talkin' about?"

"Turns out, there's still a few ranchers who haven't sold out yet. They're countin' on Hodson to get his herd through. Their thinkin' is, if only one herd can get through, then the market for Texas cows will go up."

"That's probably true," Sawyer agreed. "But with all the land Phelps has bought, you'd think he would want the market for cows to go up too. Why is he against it?"

"He wants the market to go up sometime, but not just yet," Coleman explained. "You see, the longer Phelps can keep the other ranchers down, the more land he can buy. And he's in a position where he can afford to wait for cattle prices to come back. The Texans can't. That's why he wants me to stop the drive."

"And steal the cows?"

Coleman smiled. "Tell the truth, he didn't say nothin' 'bout stealin' the cows. That's my idea."

"I see. So you figure to stop the drive, plus pick yourself up a little money on the side. Is that about right?" Sawyer asked.

"Can you blame me?" Coleman asked. "I don't believe in turning my back on opportunity."

Sawyer laughed. "Good point. All right, what do you want me to do?"

"I want you to take the entire herd. Once you have the herd, we'll sell the cows to the railroad. You can have twenty percent of the take."

"Wait a minute, I do all the work, and you only want to give me twenty percent?"

Sawyer's reaction to Coleman's offer made him want to smile, but he held the smile back. Sawyer had said, ". . . you want to give me twenty percent." To Coleman, it meant that Sawyer had already conceded proprietary rights of the herd to Coleman.

"I brought the cows to you," Coleman explained. "And I planned the operation. If it weren't for me, you'd still be sitting here wondering where the buffalo are."

"I won't do it for less than thirty percent," Sawyer said.

"It's my operation. What makes you think I should give you that much of it?"

"I'm going to have to get some men together, and they'll need to be paid," Sawyer said. "With nine drovers watchin' the herd, I can't do it by myself, even if half of 'em is women."

"You'll pay the men out of your share?" Coleman asked.

"Yeah," Sawyer agreed.

"All right, I feel like I'm being robbed, but I'll give you thirty percent."

"Then it's a done deal," Sawyer said.

Coleman could scarcely contain his glee. He needed the drive stopped in whatever way it took to get the job done. He had been prepared to offer as much as sixty percent to take care of them.

With negotiations between the two men completed, Sawyer called several of the other men over to him. And there, in the Mudflats Saloon, he laid out the plans for stealing the herd.

"There's a hundred dollars apiece for you

fellas," Sawyer told them. "A hundred dollars and all you have to do is take candy from a baby."

"What'll we do with the beeves once we have them?"

"We'll drive 'em up to the nearest railroad and sell 'em, same as we would buffs. Only, we won't have to slaughter and butcher them the way we would buffalo."

"A hundred dollars isn't enough."

"All right, a hundred and fifty dollars each," Sawyer promised. "But I can't pay nobody till I get the money from the railroad."

The men all agreed that for the extra fifty dollars, they would wait for their pay. What they didn't know was they would have had to wait for their pay anyway, as Sawyer was as broke as any of them.

"So, what do we do now?"

"For now, nothing," Sawyer answered. "Just hang around here until I call you. I've got some plans to make."

Some of the men stepped up to the bar for another drink, but several of them got into a poker game, playing for markers that would be redeemable after they were paid for the job they would be doing for Emil Sawyer.

One man didn't join the others. Tall, and thin almost to the point of emaciation, Ollie

Turner sat in one corner of the saloon eating his beans and nursing one beer — one beer was all he could afford. If anyone could have used the money Sawyer was offering, it was Turner. For the last two years, Turner, formerly a member of the Texas Twenty-fifth Field Artillery, had been a prisoner of war at the camp in Elmyra, New York. New York was a long way off, and it had taken him three months to make it this far on his way back home to San Antonio, Texas.

Despite the fact that he needed money, he had no intention of taking Sawyer up on his offer. He had fought for Texas and Texans for better than four years. He wasn't about to fight against them now.

As Ollie left the saloon, three more men arrived, tying their horses to the long hitching rail in front of the saloon.

These three men were as disreputable looking as any of the men inside. They looked like outlaws, and Ollie had no doubt but that they were. As Mudflats had no government, and thus no law, it was an ideal gathering place for such hard men.

Ollie untied his own horse as he looked down the rail at the other mounts. For a moment, he considered stealing one of the other horses. He had worked his way this far by doing odd jobs, barely scraping together enough money to buy a nag that was a suitable candidate for the glue factory. He literally didn't know how much farther this horse would take him.

If he did steal one of the horses, he would be willing to bet that it wouldn't be the first time the horse had been stolen. The temptation was great, but Ollie was a Texan by birth, and ingrained deep inside him was the stigma that being a horse thief carried. Of all the evils, horse thievery ranked near the very top of Ollie's list of sins, and he couldn't bring himself to become one, no matter how badly he needed a horse, no matter that the chances were very good that if he took one of these horses, he wouldn't be taking it from the rightful owner.

Nearly as high on Ollie's list of personal sins was cattle rustling. Though what Sawyer and Coleman were planning had nothing to do with him, he didn't like the idea of a couple of Yankees stealing from fellow Texans. Especially if, as they had indicated, the leader of the group of Texans had been a soldier and a prisoner of war. Because of his own experience as a prisoner of war, Ollie felt a strong kinship toward the man, even though they had never met.

It was that feeling of kinship that caused

Ollie to do something that was completely out of the ordinary for him: He decided to stick his nose into someone else's business. He would tell the Texans about the plan being formulated to steal their herd. It wouldn't be hard to find them. If they were coming from Texas, they would have to be to the south, and a herd of three thousand cows should be easy enough to spot.

It was nearly suppertime when Opal spotted the rider coming toward the camp. Because she was still concerned that Dane Coleman might be coming after her, she was more alert than most of the others. So when she saw the rider approaching, she felt a moment of apprehension. The fear passed quickly, however, when she realized that the man coming toward them wasn't Coleman.

"Dick," she called. "Someone's coming." She pointed toward the north.

"Anybody you know?" Dick asked.

Opal shook her head.

"If he was looking for trouble, I don't think he'd ride in like this," Dick said. "But everyone be on the alert, just the same."

"Hello the camp," the rider hailed.

"Come on in," Dick invited.

They studied the rider as he approached. He was bony and angular, almost to the point of emaciation.

"We're just sittin' to supper," Dick said. "You're welcome to join us."

"Thanks," the rider said as he dismounted. He pulled out his own mess kit and handed it to Kitty. The rider studied the group through eyes that Dick had seen many times before. They were the eyes of a man who had seen too much suffering and death. They were the eyes of someone who had seen the horrors of war close up. He had the flat, glazed look of others he had seen at the prisoner of war camp.

"Where were you held?" Dick asked knowingly.

"Elmyra," the rider answered, showing no surprise that Dick had asked the question. "What about you?"

"Camp Robinson, Illinois."

For a moment the two men connected on a plane that was much closer and more personal than anything Dick shared with those with whom he had been riding for the last several weeks.

The rider stuck his hand out. "The name is Ollie Turner," he said.

Dick introduced himself, then the others. Kitty handed Ollie his plate, and he began to eat like a man to whom food had been a scarce item for much of the last few years.

"Thank you, ma'am, this is mighty tasty," Ollie said between gulping mouthfuls. He looked at Dick. "You the leader of this group?"

"Yes."

"Well, I ain't just passin' through. I got news you folks prob'ly need to hear."

"What sort of news?" Marline asked.

"Do any of you know a short, kinda heavyset, bald-headed man? This here fella's got no hair a'tall, not on top of his head, not even any eyebrows."

"Dane Coleman," Opal spat.

"Yeah, we know the son of a bitch," Ron said. "What about him?"

"He's back in Mudflats right now makin' plans with a fella by the name of Emil Sawyer. They're making plans to hit your herd."

"Let 'em try," Buck said boastfully. "Coleman already spooked 'em into a stampede once, and we got it stopped. That was before the cows had water, too. I think it would be a lot harder to get 'em stampeded now."

"They ain't talkin' 'bout stampedin'," Ollie said. "They talkin' 'bout stealin' the herd."

"Steal it?" Ron said. "Why on earth would anyone want to steal a herd when there's cows for the taking, just running wild?"

"I reckon they just don't want to take the time and effort to hunt wild cows, especially if there is already a herd put together," Ollie said.

"How do just two of them plan on doing this?" Dooley asked.

Ollie shook his head. "Well, that's the other thing. There's a lot more than two of them. Must be fifteen or twenty people back there who have agreed to join them."

"When do they plan on hitting us?" Dick asked.

"Near as I could make out, they figure about midmorning tomorrow," Ollie answered.

As everyone began talking about how they should handle the news Ollie just brought them, Opal poured Ollie a second cup of coffee.

"Is it true that all you folks put your cows together to make this herd?" Ollie asked.

"Well, they did," Opal explained, nodding toward the others. "But none of them are my cows. I'm just riding with them."

"Is that a fact? Then I reckon you must be the whore they was talkin' about," Ollie said.

There was a sudden gasp from the group, then everyone looked at Ollie with an expression of disapproval.

Noticing his faux pax, Ollie began to

189

stutter. "Look, I . . . I'm sorry, I don't mean nothin' by it," he apologized quickly. "I reckon I sort of lost all sense of decency, what with the war and prison and all. I ask you folks to please forgive me."

"We aren't the ones to ask for forgiveness," Ron said purposefully. "It's up to Miss Opal whether or not she wants to forgive you."

"It's all right," Opal said quickly, defusing the momentary tension. "I was a whore, and I guess once a person is a whore they always are, for all that they might try to get away from it."

"Well, ma'am, if you say you ain't a whore anymore, then you ain't," Ollie said. "And, like I say, I apologize to all, and especially to you, if I caused any disquiet."

"With that all settled, that brings up the question as to what we're going to do about these men who want to steal our herd," Marline said.

"How many men did you say would likely be with Coleman?" Dick asked.

"There's at least fifteen to twenty men back there in the saloon," Ollie said. "And I figure nearly all of 'em will throw in with 'im."

"Are you telling me that everyone in that town will join Coleman?" Dick asked.

"I reckon they will," Ollie said. "You gotta

understand that Mudflats ain't no regular town. From the way they was talkin' while I was there, I gather that nobody goes there without a reason, and nine times out of ten, the reason they do is because they're up to no good. You see, what with no law an' all, Mudflats is a good place for outlaws to be."

"What are we going to do, Dick?" Dooley asked. "We can't fight fifteen or twenty men."

"Give me a moment to think about it," Dick answered.

"Yeah, give him time, Dooley. Dick will come up with something," Buck said assuredly.

"They're going to do this tomorrow morning, you say?" Dick asked Ollie.

"About midmorning. Leastwise, that's the way I understood it," Ollie said. "'Course you got to know that I was listening from my table over at the edge of the room. I didn't want to be a part of what they were planning."

Dick smiled. "Good, that'll give us time."

"You have an idea?" Marline asked.

"I have three thousand ideas," Dick answered.

Dick's answer made no sense at all, and everyone stared at him as if he had suddenly lost his mind.

Chapter Fourteen

The Driscoll Ranch
Hutchinson County, Texas

Reba Driscoll carried a lighted candle down the hall toward her bedroom. She checked on her two young sons, Paul, twelve, and Eddie, eleven, and saw that they were sleeping peacefully. Then she reflexively looked into Priscilla's room, even though Priscilla was gone.

She was not surprised that she had checked on Priscilla, for she had instinctively checked Perry's room for almost a year after he left for the war. She didn't quit until his absence had become permanent, when she learned he was killed at Antietam. She prayed to God that no such thing would happen to Priscilla, and that she would come back safely to them.

Both Giles and Reba would have preferred that Priscilla had not undertaken the long and treacherous drive to distant Dakota Territory. Had they known about it beforehand they would have done everything in their power to stop her. But even if they had tried to stop her, Reba wasn't sure they could have. Priscilla was a very determined young woman and may well have gone on the drive with or without their permission.

On the other hand, by leaving as she did, the two youngest children were caught as much by surprise as Reba and Giles had been. And that was a good thing, because had Paul and Eddie known about their older sister's plans, they may well have left, too, sneaking off before anyone, even Priscilla, had realized what had happened. Reba didn't think she could handle it if all her children were gone.

"Priscilla is a resourceful and self-reliant young woman," Giles had said by way of comforting Reba. "She can take care of herself. And I must confess that, now that she has embarked on this venture, I am happy that she did it."

"You can't mean that," Reba had replied.

"Yes, I do. She is doing this to save the ranch, Reba. Not only for us, but for herself, and for Paul and Eddie. I tell you this — I am proud of my daughter, as proud of her as I was of Perry when he left for the war."

"Oh, please, God, don't let them share the same fate," Reba had said as tears sprang to her eyes.

"Honey, just because Perry didn't come back, doesn't mean that Priscilla won't. And I make no apologies about comparing the two of them, for I can't separate my love, nor my pride in them."

"I know," Reba had said. "I am very proud of her, too."

Because of Priscilla's endeavor, Giles was sleeping more soundly now than he had before she left. Before, the likelihood of losing the ranch to Bryan Phelps was very real. Now, with the potential of an income being generated by Priscilla selling their cattle to a more receptive market, there was a good chance that the ranch could be saved.

Reba got undressed, put on her nightgown, then blew out the candle and slipped into bed beside her husband. Even though Giles was asleep, he sensed Reba beside him, and he accommodated his body to her presence. Within a few moments, Reba's soft snores joined Giles'.

A group of horsemen, eerily illuminated by the flickering torches many of them were carrying, appeared on the crest of the hill that overlooked the Driscoll Ranch. Bryan

Phelps, the leader of the group, looked down on the little collection of neat buildings.

"All right, boys, you know what to do," Phelps said.

One of the riders chuckled. "Damn, this is just like it was during the war."

"As far as you're concerned, this is war," Phelps said. "By sending some of their cows out of Texas, they have violated the law. That means they are criminals, and we will treat them as such. And as the duly appointed administrator for the Federal Commission of Agriculture and Livestock, I hereby deputize each and everyone of you. Remember that whatever you do here tonight, you are doing under the protection of the law of the land. Now, let's go."

The deputies rode quickly down the hill to the Driscoll Ranch. A couple of the riders broke away from the rest of the pack and headed toward the barn. One of them tossed a torch inside the barn, where it landed on dry hay. The other threw his torch up onto the dry-shake shingles of the roof. Within moments the barn was ablaze.

"Shall we bang on the door, Colonel?" one of the riders asked.

"No need," Phelps replied, sitting quietly in his saddle. "They'll come running out soon enough."

For nearly two minutes, Bryan Phelps and his ten deputies sat silently, staring at the house, their faces glowing orange in the flickering flames of the burning barn.

As the popping, snapping fire grew in heat and intensity, the horses and cows trapped inside the barn realized their danger and began screaming in terror. Phelps reached down to pat the neck of his own horse reassuringly, for the animal was very nervous at being that close to the blaze and began to prance about.

They waited.

Then, from inside the house, they heard a young voice call the alarm.

"Pa! Ma! Wake up! Wake up! The barn's aburnin'!"

Paul's shouts awakened Reba, and she poked her husband awake. When Giles opened his eyes, he didn't have to ask what was wrong, for by now the light from the burning barn lit up the bedroom as bright as day.

"What in the world! How did that happen? Reba, get the buckets. Paul, Eddie, turn out, boys! We've got to save the animals."

Giles and his two sons dashed out through the front door in their sleeping gowns, not bothering to take time to get dressed. They hurried down from the front porch, then were brought to an immediate halt by the sight of nearly a dozen men. Backlit by the burning barn, they looked as if they were ghost riders from the depths of hell. Giles shielded his eyes against the glare of the fire, but even though he stared hard at the riders, he couldn't make out any of their features.

"What the . . . who are you?" Giles demanded.

"Giles Driscoll, you are in violation of the federal law of reconstruction," Phelps said.

"Phelps, is that you? Yes, I recognize your voice," Giles said, still trying to make out features in the shadows and flickering flames.

Reba arrived on the front porch at that moment, carrying three buckets. When she saw the frightening array of men around her husband and sons, she didn't know who or what they were, but she knew the situation was no good.

"Oh, my God!" she gasped, covering her mouth with her hand. The wooden buckets fell to the porch with a clatter.

"Reba, get my gun!" Giles shouted. "Hurry, woman, my gun!"

"Giles Driscoll, you are resisting arrest," Phelps called out.

"You're damn right I'm resisting," Giles replied, starting back up onto the porch. "I'm going to blow you all to hell!"

At that moment several shots rang out, though who fired them wasn't certain. Reba saw the back of Giles' sleeping gown splatter crimson with the blood of three bullet wounds. Giles fell across the front steps, his head on the porch, his feet still on the ground. The life was already gone from his gaping eyes.

"Papa!" Eddie shouted.

"No! My God, no!" Reba screamed. She ran to her husband. "You've killed him!"

"I had no wish to kill him, Mrs. Driscoll," Phelps said. "I only intended to arrest him. He brought this on himself by resisting arrest. We all heard him, he was going for his gun."

"Murderers!" Reba shouted. "I'll go to the law and you will all hang for this."

"No, Mrs. Driscoll, we won't," Phelps replied. "Because you see, I *am* the law."

Mudflats, Kansas

The sun was barely above the eastern horizon. The early morning light picked up the blanket of dew on the meadow and flashed back in a million sparkling points of color. From their position on the crest of a hill, Dick and Ollie stared down at the little settlement of Mudflats.

"You're sure there are no women or children here?" Dick asked.

"Nary a one. I wasn't there too long, but I learned that there ain't nobody here permanent, except Ike Horner," Ollie said. "He runs the saloon and tradin' post."

Ron rode up to where the two men were standing overlooking Mudflats, then he dismounted and joined them.

"Looks kind of peaceful, don't it?" Ron asked.

"Yeah, they are going to get a surprise, all right," Ollie said.

"Is everyone ready?" Dick asked.

Ron nodded. "We're all ready." He giggled. "A few days ago we just about broke our necks trying to stop a stampede. Now we're planning on gettin' one agoin'."

"The herd is well watered and well fed," Ollie said. "I doubt they'll run too far."

"Let's just hope they run far enough," Dick replied. He swung into his saddle. "All right, let's do it."

Dick, Ollie, and Ron rode back to join the others. All were mounted except Kitty. She had left much earlier that morning, taking the wagon to the place where they planned to rendezvous. The only movement within the herd came from those few animals who, sensing that it was time to be underway again, were walking around as if expending nervous energy. But even they would make no effort to move until urged to do so, for with the water and graze that was available, the herd would remain indefinitely if not prodded.

The drovers moved their mounts into position behind the herd. The women had blankets in their hands, and the men were holding loaded revolvers. When all were in position, they looked toward Dick in expectation.

There was a long moment of waiting as Dick held his hand up. Then he brought it down sharply. "Now!" he shouted.

Almost immediately after his shout, Ron, Buck, Dooley, and Ollie fired their pistols into the air. The women began waving blankets, and the herd, startled by the sudden fury of noise and activity, broke into a rapid, lumbering gait.

"Yee-hah! Yee-hah!" Dick shouted at the top of his voice, riding back and forth behind the herd, waving his hat at them to urge them into a faster run.

Inside the Mudflats saloon, the floor, tables, and chairs were filled with motionless patrons. In anticipation of their planned activity for the next day, several bottles of whiskey had been consumed last night, and this morning the men were sleeping off a drunk.

Ike Horner was the only one who was already awake. He was also the only one who had slept in a bed last night, because this was where he lived.

Horner had come across the abandoned buildings of Mudflats some two years earlier while the war was still on. Horner was a civilian contract teamster, taking a wagonload of army supplies to Fort Larned, Kansas. Instead of completing his journey, however, he stopped at Mudflats, unloaded the wagon, and using the army goods to trade with the Indians, went into business for himself. He had been right here, in this same spot, gouging buffalo hunters, Indians, and travelers ever since.

Mudflats was a natural stopping place for army deserters, thieves, murderers, and anyone else on the run, because it was out of the way, it had no law, and it was the only place where such people could drink and feel safe. No one ever complained about the overpriced, overwatered whiskey, because they had no other place to go, and they were glad enough to be able to get anything.

Horner gave a passing thought to cooking breakfast for his "patrons," but decided that so many of them had drunk themselves into a stupor the night before that they probably wouldn't be interested in buying breakfast. And that was too bad because without breakfast, there was very little way to get any extra money from them. Perhaps he could charge them a quarter apiece for spending the night in the saloon.

Almost as soon as he thought of the idea, he abandoned it. He knew that none of them would stay if they had to pay. They would just move outside, and he would lose some of the income he made from liquor. He decided to put on a pot of coffee, then smiled as the idea came to him. Because of their hangovers, many of them would be wanting a cup, and he could sell coffee for as much as he would get for an entire breakfast. Overall, coffee would be cheaper and much less work.

He ground the beans, then put the water on to boil. After that was taken care of, he stepped outside to relieve himself.

At first, Horner thought the sound he heard was a distant, rolling thunder. As there wasn't a cloud in the sky, thunder seemed unlikely. Then, looking to the south, he saw something that first puzzled, and then startled him.

It was cattle! An entire herd of cattle was running hellbent across the plains! He looked at them for a moment, unable to believe his eyes. Then he realized that they weren't just running, they were stampeding, and they were heading right for him.

"What the hell?" he asked, quietly. Then shock gave way to panic as he realized that he was in danger. "My God, my God, it's a stampede! Stampede!" he shouted at the top of his voice. He ran back into the saloon. "Stampede!" he shouted again.

"Horner, what the hell are you carrying on about?" Sawyer asked, sleepily. Sawyer had pulled two of the tables together and was lying across them with his hat over his face.

"Cattle!" Horner said. "Thousands of them! They're coming right for us."

"What do you mean?" Coleman asked irritably, lying on the floor, near the bar.

"I . . . I . . . Look for yourselves!" Horner shouted, unable to make it any clearer than he already had.

"Have you gone loco?" Sawyer asked. He got up from the table and walked over to look through the window. The herd was less than one hundred yards away. The only wooden structure, the outhouse on the outskirts of the settlement, went down under the onslaught of thundering hooves.

"Holy shit!" Sawyer shouted.

Sawyer's shout alerted the rest of the men, though his warning wasn't really necessary, for it was obvious by now to even the most hungover of all the sleepers.

"We've got to get out of here!" someone shouted, running toward the door.

"Bailey, you fool! Get back in here!" Sawyer yelled, but his warning went unheeded. Bailey ran outside, and immediately found himself trapped in an ocean of cattle crashing toward him. He tried to get back to the relative safety of the saloon but it was too late. He was run down and crushed by the stampeding cows.

Those inside the saloon shuddered in terror as the ground shook around them. Now and again, the horns of one of the bolting steers would hook into the crusted adobe walls of the building, gouging out large chunks of mud and dirt. With a crash, the windowframe was pulled out, leaving a large, gaping hole in the wall. Through the hole, the terrified men could see a seemingly unending stream of wild-eyed cattle.

One corner of the wall came tumbling down, bringing the roof down with it. The men inside screamed, and fell to the floor with their arms over their heads. They gritted their teeth and cried in fear and felt the earth shake as the herd continued to rumble by. Finally the shaking stopped and the sound began to recede.

Finally, it was quiet.

"What . . . what the hell was that?" someone asked.

"I've never heard of cows stampeding through a town like that," another added.

"They weren't stampeded through the town," Sawyer said. "They were drove through the town."

"What?"

"I saw them, riding behind the herd, urging them on. Them cows was drove through here on purpose. Those sons of bitches tried to kill us."

"That's the kids and women we're supposed to take the candy from?" one of the men asked.

"Yeah," Sawyer answered.

"Seems to me like it ain't goin' to be all that easy."

"Come on," Coleman growled. "Let's go get 'em now."

"How you planning on doing that?" one of the men asked.

"What do you mean how are we going to

do it? We'll just chase the bastards down, that's how we'll do it," Coleman answered.

Sawyer walked over to look through the large hole in the wall.

"We ain't goin' to get far without horses," he said, dryly.

"What?" Coleman asked.

"There ain't no horses," Sawyer repeated. "I see a couple of 'em lyin' out there dead, along with that damn fool, Bailey. But the rest of 'em's gone."

Coleman, Sawyer, Horner, and the others went outside to look around. The outhouse and the smaller of the two warehouses were completely demolished. The larger warehouse and the saloon were badly damaged, with collapsed roofs and great, gaping holes in the walls.

"Oh, I'm ruined," Horner lamented. "I'm ruined."

"Damn if it don't look like this place has been shelled by cannon fire," Sawyer said as he surveyed the damage.

A couple of the men went over to examine the body of the man who had run out of the building in panic.

"Ol' Bailey here's flatter'n a flapjack," one of them called back to Sawyer. "What do you think we ought to do with 'im?"

"Do with 'im?" Sawyer replied. "What do

you mean, do with 'im?"

"Well, I mean, should we bury him or what?"

"Bury him or not, it don't matter none to me," Sawyer said. He started walking.

"Where you going?" Coleman called after him.

"To find a horse," Sawyer answered. "They can't all have run away."

"What about the ones who did this? You just goin' to let 'em get away with it?"

"Ain't my problem," Sawyer answered. "Hell, I told you from the start, I didn't want nothin' to do with no damn cows."

"What about the money we were going to get from selling the cows?"

Sawyer hawked up a spit before he answered Coleman. "Like I said, Coleman, this ain't none of my concern," he said. "But seems to me like the smartest thing you could do is let 'em go ahead and sell the cows . . . then you just take the money from 'em. Stealin' money is a whole lot easier than stealin' cows."

Coleman blinked a couple of times at the beautiful simplicity of it. That was it! What Sawyer said was absolutely right! Why hadn't he thought of that before? There was no sense in him breaking his back trying to stop them. If they fail, then his job is done.

And if they succeed, then all he has to do is take the money from them.

"See you around," Sawyer said as he walked off.

"Yeah," Coleman replied. "I'll see you around."

The stampeding herd ran another three miles before slowing to a trot and finally halting.

"Yahoo!" Buck shouted, grinning broadly and slapping his thigh with his hat. "Did you see what we did to that place?"

"That was something!" Dooley said. "Lord, I've never had so much fun in my life."

As the others blustered about, Ollie dismounted and started patting his horse on the neck. The animal was covered with lather and its sides were heaving as it gasped for air. Though no one else had noticed it before, everyone realized that Ollie's horse was in extreme distress.

"How is he?" Dick asked.

"I'm afraid he's done for," Ollie replied. Even as he spoke, the horse made a few more audible gasps, then sunk to his knees and fell onto its side. It twitched a few more times, then was still.

The others dismounted and came over to

look down at the horse. The expressions on their faces reflected their pity for the poor creature.

"Did you have him long?" Opal asked.

Ollie shook his head. "Not too long. I bought him in Cincinnati. He was headed for the glue factory and I paid twenty dollars for him. Folks laughed at me, said he wouldn't take me ten miles, but he brought me all the way here. Turns out he was a pretty noble creature, and I'm afraid I didn't do right by him."

"You did right by him," Opal replied. "If you hadn't come along, he would've been dead long before now. You not only gave him a longer life, you gave him a purpose. And take it from someone who knows: Without a purpose, life is barely worth living. I'd be willing to bet that he was thankful to you everyday."

"You think so?" Ollie asked.

"I'm sure of it," Opal said.

"I thank you for that. It comforts me some. But it still leaves me without a horse."

"Not for long," Dick said. "When we came through Mudflats several of the horses got loose. I can see a couple of them in the field down there right now. Why don't we just go down there and get you one?"

"You think that would be all right?" Ollie

asked. "I wouldn't want to be hung for a horse thief."

Dick laughed. "Trust me, Ollie, I don't think any of the men we left back there are going to go to the law, claiming we stole a horse from them."

"Come on, Buck, let's go get him one," Anita shouted and, with a laugh, urged her horse into a gallop. Caught by surprise, Buck rode hard to catch up with her, and the others watched the two as they galloped down the long slope, the hooves of their horses throwing up clumps of mud and grass.

"I've got a hunch those two will pick you out a good one," Dick said.

Windom, Texas

Carter Nunlee, the undertaker, had learned his trade during the war. He became so skilled at restoring battle-damaged soldiers to a state fit to be viewed by their grieving family members that he achieved a well-deserved degree of fame. Now, when he had a project of which he was particularly proud, he would display the body on a catafalque just inside the big glass window on the front of his funeral home.

Word began to spread through the town that Giles Driscoll would soon be on display. As a result, a crowd gathered outside the window. Some were friends, here out of genuine grief, others were local businessmen here out of respect. But a sizable number had gathered from unabashed curiosity.

As if opening the curtain on a staged drama, Nunlee pulled back the drapes so his work could be seen. Then he stepped outside, beaming proudly as he listened to the accolades for his work.

"Don't he look natural?" someone asked.

"The color's good."

"Looks just like he's sleepin'."

The public showing lasted only until Reba Driscoll and her two sons arrived in town, driving a wagon that was filled with all their belongings. Seeing her husband on display, the lady, dressed in black for the occasion, put a stop to the show. She began berating a perplexed Carter Nunlee, who had thought she would be pleased with what he was doing.

Nunlee, who had done such a good job in preparing the body, was somewhat offended when Reba Driscoll didn't take the black and silver casket, but chose a simple pine coffin instead. He was further offended when she didn't want to pay the five dollars extra he would have charged for using the glass-sided hearse. As a result, the body was borne through the streets of the town and to the cemetery in the back of a buckboard.

Although there was no church service, it had been arranged that the preacher would say his words by the graveside out at the cemetery. John and Delia Hodson were among those who attended the funeral, and they stood with Joel and Trudy Konda, looking on sadly as Reba, Paul, and Eddie sat on chairs alongside the open grave. Caleb and Roberta Blackburn were there, too, as were Ellis and Wanda Votaw, Odell and Mary Sietz, and Ben and Ethyl Winters.

As soon as the coffin was lowered into the grave, Father Jason McKenzie of St. Paul's Episcopal Church stepped up to it and began to speak in a clarion voice that carried throughout the entire cemetery.

"For as much as it hath pleased Almighty God, in His wise providence, to take out of the world the soul of Giles Driscoll, we therefore commit his body to the ground."

Reba, Paul, and Eddie got up from their chairs and stepped up to the grave. Each of them dropped a handful of dirt onto the coffin. They stood there for a moment, looking down into the grave, then, at a nod from Father McKenzie, sat down again. McKenzie completed his prayer.

"Earth to earth, ashes to ashes, dust to dust; looking for the general Resurrection in the last day, and the life of the world to come, through our Lord Jesus Christ; at whose second coming in glorious majesty to judge the world, the earth and the sea shall give up their dead; and the corruptible bodies of those who sleep in Him shall be changed, and made like unto His own glorious body; according to the mighty working whereby He is able to subdue all things unto Himself."

Reba's friends and neighbors had brought food, and after the service was concluded, they all gathered under a nearby tree. Here, a long table was spread with baked ham, fried chicken, potato salad, corn, beans, biscuits, pies and cakes, enough to feed half the town. The gathering quickly turned into a picnic atmosphere, and several children began playing tag among the tombstones.

"I wish you wouldn't leave, Reba," Trudy said. "Why, you are one of my oldest and dearest friends. Our families came to this valley together, right after Texas got its independence from Mexico."

"Can't we talk you out of it?" John asked. "Think of Priscilla, off on this drive. I just know she's going to come back with enough money to run your ranch for another year. She is going to be sorely disappointed to find that you have sold out."

"Yes, and think of Paul and Eddie," Caleb Blackburn said. "Don't you feel that you owe it to them to hang on to the ranch until they are old enough to run it?"

"You heard what happened at the inquest into Giles' murder?" Reba asked.

Those who were trying to talk Reba into staying looked at the ground in discomfort.

"Yes, we heard," Joel Konda said. "It was ruled justifiable homicide by reason of self-defense."

"Self-defense," Reba said in contempt. "He was shot in the back. But all ten of Phelps' so-called deputies swore that Giles was going for his gun. Yes, he was going for it, but it was in the house, and he was outside."

"I've written a letter to the state capitol," John said. "But since the war, I'm not sure we even have any state officials. I'm afraid the state government is in the hands of the federal authorities, just like it is here."

"Not every federal official will be as bad as Bryan Phelps," Trudy suggested. "Surely there is justice, somewhere."

"For me, it's too late for justice," Reba said.

"Where will you go?" Joel asked.

"I have a sister in Fort Worth," Reba answered. "I sent her a letter, telling her what happened. We'll be staying with her family for a while."

"What about the ranch?"

"What about it? It belongs to Phelps now."

"You mean you've already sold your ranch to him?" Joel Konda asked in surprise.

"I have. I sold it for fifteen hundred dollars in gold."

"How could you have done that? How could you have sold your ranch to the very man who killed your husband?"

"Don't you judge me, Joel Konda," Reba replied. "I needed that money. I needed it desperately."

"We would've worked something out."

"How were we going to work something out? Could you have given me fifteen hundred dollars in gold?"

"Well, no, but —"

"There are no buts," Reba replied. "What's done is done, and my children and I must get on with our lives. Besides, do you know how long it has been since we have seen that kind of money?"

Joel pinched the bridge of his nose and

sighed. "I suppose you did what you felt you had to do," he said. "But I ask you again, have you given any thought to Priscilla? What is she going to think when she gets back?"

Reba shook her head. "All I can do is pray that she will understand. Oh, and Trudy, I've written a letter to her. Would you give it to her when she returns?"

"Yes, of course I will," Trudy replied.

"Ma," Paul called. "Come on. If we want to make it to the Pattersons' by nightfall, we need to get amovin'."

"I'm coming," Reba said, getting up from her chair and reaching for her veil. "Listen to him give orders, bless his heart," she said quietly to those who were gathered around her. "He's already beginning to take charge of things. Paul feels like every bit of the responsibility is on his shoulders now."

"He's a good boy, and I know he'll live up to his expectations," Joel said.

"Yes, he is. Both of them are good boys. They lost their big brother, then their father. They've already gone through more tragedy than anyone their age should have to see."

"Adversity destroys some people," Joel said. "But it strengthens others. I think Paul and Eddie will be strengthened."

"I hope that you are right," Reba said,

walking toward the wagon where Paul and Eddie were waiting patiently for her. Those who were still at the cemetery watched as the two boys helped their mother climb onto the wagon, then climb on themselves. Paul released the wagon brake, snapped the reins over the back of the team, and the heavily loaded wagon lurched forward.

"Poor woman," Trudy said as the wagon left the cemetery. "I hope she can find some peace."

Joel sighed. "I do, too," he said. "But I wish she hadn't sold her ranch."

"What's done is done," Trudy said. "And that's the end of it."

"No, unfortunately, what's done is just the beginning of it."

"What are you talking about?" Trudy asked, confused by her husband's strange statement.

"Trudy, the headwaters of McCamey Creek are on the Driscoll ranch. McCamey Creek furnishes more than half the water for the Tilting K."

"Oh," Trudy I said. "That could be bad, couldn't it?"

"If Phelps decides to dam the creek, it sure could be bad."

"But he couldn't do that," Trudy said. "There's a law against diverting water. Remember? We were going to divert one of the creeks to bring water to the east range."

"That was a state law," Joel explained. "Phelps is the Federal Administrator for Agriculture and Livestock. Federal, Trudy. That means he can override any state law he wants to."

CHAPTER FIFTEEN

"Boss! Boss, wake up! We got troubles."

Joel Konda fought against the intrusion into his sleep, but the persistent voice continued, and was joined by a banging on the bedroom door.

"Boss, you awake?" the voice called through the closed door.

Joel groaned once, and sat up.

"Joel, what is it?" Trudy asked.

"I don't know. Sounds like Pete."

"Boss? Boss, you awake?"

"Yeah, just a minute," Joel replied groggily.

The weather had been menacing when Joel went to bed, and now it was living up to its threat. A hard, driving rain drummed against the roof and the window. A flash of lightning illuminated the bedroom.

Joel lit a candle, then moved to the bedroom door and pulled it open. "What time is it?" Joel asked.

"It lacks a little of being midnight, I reckon," Pete answered.

"Let me get dressed," Joel said. He knew that Pete wouldn't wake him at this time of the night unless there was a legitimate reason.

"What is it?" Trudy asked, sleepily.

"I don't know yet," Joel said. "But whatever it is, I'll deal with it. You go on back to sleep." Joel dressed quickly, then stepped out into the hall. "What's up?" he asked.

"It started rainin' a couple of hours ago," Pete said. "And I remembered that I had me a couple of wolf skins staked out and curin', so I figured I'd better ride out and get 'em afore they got ruint. That's when I seen it. I told George about it, and he got up, got dressed, and went down there to take a look. He said I should bring you right away."

"All right, I don't suppose you are going to tell me anything until I see for myself," Joel said. "So, I may as well quit asking."

The two men ran quickly through the rain to the barn, where Joel selected a mount and saddled him. Pete's horse, already saddled and still wet from the downpour, stood by the manger calmly cropping hay. A moment later, Joel, mounted and wearing his poncho, rode to the front of the barn where Pete was waiting in the relative dryness of the barn. "All right," Joel said, reaching down to give his horse a reassuring pat. "Let's go see what you've got to show me."

As the two men rode through the rain it slashed against them and ran in cold rivulets off the folds and creases of their ponchos. It blew in sheets across the trail in front of them, and pounded wickedly into the wind-whipped trees and bushes. The lightning, when it flashed, lit up the landscape in stark, harsh white against featureless black shadow. The flashes were followed immediately by thunder, snapping shrilly at first, then rolling through the valleys, picking up the resonance of the hollows in an echoing boom.

They didn't have to speak during the ride; in fact conversation would have been difficult if not impossible. Besides, Pete, by his action, had already indicated that he was going to show Joel something which spoke louder than words, and therefore Joel was willing to wait.

After a mile or two, they overtook George who, to Joel's surprise, wasn't riding, but was driving a buckboard. In the back of the buckboard there was something under a tarpaulin. Joel pulled the canvas back and saw two kegs.

"What are you doing with that?" Joel

221

asked, pointing to the kegs. "That looks like the blasting powder we use to go after stumps."

"Yes, sir, that's what it is, all right," George said. "Only we ain't goin' after no stumps."

"What's going on here?"

"Come over here, Mr. Konda," Pete said. Pete had ridden several feet off the road. "Take a look at this, and you'll know what we're talking about."

Joel responded to Pete's summons.

"Look down there," Pete invited.

"What am I looking at? McCamey Creek?" Joel asked. "What about it, it's . . . hey, wait a minute! With this rain, it should be much higher than that."

"Yes, sir, that was my thinkin', too," Pete said. "I found it to be a pure puzzlement as to why the creek wasn't about to spill over its banks, so I got to checkin', and you can't believe what I found."

"What did you find?"

"Mr. Konda, that there ain't flowin' creek water you're lookin' at. It's rain water, no different from any mud puddle after a rain. Soon as the rain stops, it'll go back down. They done dammed up the creek over at the Driscoll place."

Sighing, Joel shook his head. "I was afraid

they might wind up doing something like that."

"We can take care of it right now," Pete said. "Just give me 'n George the word, and we'll go over there and blow it up."

"What good would that do?" Joel asked. "Phelps would just build again."

"If they do, we'll blow it up again," Pete said. "We can blow it up a hell of a lot faster'n they can build it."

Joel stroked his chin for a moment as he considered Pete's proposition, then he nodded. "All right," he said. "Let's do it. It won't really accomplish anything, but I'd much rather go out with a bang than with a whisper."

"Now you're talkin', Mr. Konda," Pete said, smiling broadly.

Returning to the road, the three men continued north along the bed of what used to be McCamey Creek. Along the way, it stopped raining, and a surprisingly bright moon peeked out from behind a large fluffy, silver cloud. Mud puddles and rivulets of water reflected the glow of the moon and sent slivers of silver scattering through the night.

When they reached the rail fence that marked the line between the Tilting K and the Driscoll Ranch, they saw that the road that connected the two ranches had been barricaded.

"What the hell? When did that go up?" Joel asked.

There had never been a barricade between the two ranches before. Even the fence line between the two ranches had represented no barrier, as it was more to mark the property than to protect it. In the past, the cows of both ranches had intermingled here sharing grass and water. Neither spread made any attempt to separate them until roundup time, when they would choose between them by the brands they wore. Now, a gate stretched across the road, and the gate was closed and locked.

"Bust it open, Pete," Joel ordered.

"Yes, sir!"

Pete took a small handax from the back of the wagon, and in a few quick blows, had the gate open. He climbed back onto his horse, and the wagon and two outriders moved on through.

It was almost a mile before they found the dam. Shimmering in the soft nightglow, the structure was fabricated of mud, stone, and logs, making it an effective, if not particularly attractive dam. McCamey Creek had pooled up behind the barrier and was already forming a small lake, spreading out across the range. With the rain, the lake was certain to get large very quickly.

"This is a pretty good-sized dam," Joel said. "We're not going to do any good at all if we just blow a few logs around. We have to bring the whole dam down. So let's take a look around to find a place to put the powder so it'll do the most good," Joel suggested.

For the next several minutes the three men climbed around on the dam, choosing first one place, then discarding it in favor of another. Finally, by general consensus they found a spot on the dam that all agreed would be the best place to set the charge. They returned to the wagon to get the kegs of blasting powder.

"You fellas get your hands up!" a disembodied voice called from the darkness.

Pete and George raised their hands as directed. Joel looked up toward the sound of the voice, but he could see nothing but silver and black shadows in the moonlight.

"Who's up there?" Joel called.

A rock came tumbling down the side of the hill, then another, and finally Joel could see a man appearing out of the dark, holding a rifle on them.

"You're one of Phelps' men, aren't you?"

Joel asked. "I don't know your name, but I've seen you before."

"You would be Konda, wouldn't you?" the man with the rifle asked.

"Yes."

"What are you doin' here, Konda? This ain't your land."

"No, but it is my creek. By common law, McCamey Creek belongs to everyone."

"We ain't goin' by common law now. We're goin' by Phelps' law," the rifleman said.

"You never gave me your name."

"The name's Jensen. I work for Colonel Phelps."

"As what? As his hired gun?"

The rifleman chuckled. "You might say it's somethin' like that. Mr. Phelps hired me to keep folks from doin' just exactly what you're doin'. You're trespassing on private property."

Joel pointed to the dam. "Phelps has no right damming up the creek like this."

"And you were planning on doin' somethin' about it, were you?" Jensen asked.

"If need be."

Jensen made a waving motion with his rifle. "How about the three of you backin' away from that buckboard? I want your

226

hands up and your mouths shut." As Joel and his two longtime cowboys backed away from the buckboard, Jensen started toward it. "I aim to have a look-see at what you're carrying."

"What we're carryin' is none of your business," Joel said, moving toward the wagon.

Jensen cocked his rifle and pointed it menacingly at Joel. "Maybe you didn't understand. I plan to make it my business."

Jensen stepped up to the buckboard and flipped the tarpaulin back, then he whistled under his breath. "Well now," he said. "Primer fuse and kegs of black powder. So, you ain't carryin' nothing that would interest me, huh?" He laughed. "Konda, you are one dumb son of a bitch, did you know that? Do you really think a few kegs of gunpowder would take out this dam?"

"I figured it was worth a try," Joel answered.

"And here I thought you was supposed to be so smart. Why, this powder wouldn't even make a dent in it. But I ought to let you go ahead and try, just to see the expression on your face when it doesn't work."

"All right," Joel said. "Let me try."

"Oh, yeah, you'd like that, wouldn't you? Unhitch the team and leave the buckboard and powder here. Then the three of you get off this land."

"Go ahead and unhitch the team, Pete. It don't look like we got much of a choice," George said.

"George," Pete protested.

"Do it, Pete," George said.

"I've got to hand it to you, you are smarter than you look," Jensen said to George. "You other two better pay attention to this old man."

"Who are you calling an old man?" George asked.

As Pete began unhitching the team, George stepped over to the edge of the road and looked down over the precipice, toward the dam below. Because of the earlier rain, McCamey Creek was flowing in freshet stage, the pooled water shining brightly in the moonlight. Joel stepped over and joined him.

"Boss, I didn't set the brake," George said in a quiet whisper. "Soon as the team is unhitched, if we both give it a shove, it'll go right over and crash down onto the top of the dam."

"That won't do any good," Joel whispered back.

"Yes, sir, it will," George insisted. "The top of both of them kegs is filled with nitroglycerin."

"Nitro?" Joel gasped in a harsh whisper. "Damn, George, you drove all the way out here with nitro-laced blasting powder? You're lucky you haven't already blown yourself up."

"Yes, sir, I reckon so. But like Jensen said, the powder wouldn't of done it alone."

"You two — quit your palaverin'," Jensen ordered gruffly, pointing his rifle at Joel and George.

Pete unhitched the team, then led it away from the buckboard. He and George exchanged nods, then, quickly, George and Joel stepped up to the wagon and gave it a push. It started rolling toward the drop-off.

"What the hell are you fellas doin'? Get away from there!" Jensen shouted. He fired a warning shot.

"My God!" George said, jerking back from the buckboard. "Mr. Konda, get away, the crazy son of a bitch is shooting at the wagon!"

George and Pete began to run. Joel turned to run as well, but he tripped and fell just as Jensen fired a second time. Jensen's bullet found a more volatile mark. There was a stomach-shaking boom as the nitrolaced blasting powder exploded and the wagon went into the air in hundreds of little pieces.

"Look out!" George shouted, and he dived behind a pile of rocks, followed closely by Pete. Mushrooming dust and smoke hung above them for several seconds, then began drifting away.

"George," a pained voice called.

"Mr. Konda!" George replied, getting up and looking around. "Mr. Konda, where are you?"

"I'm over here," Joel replied, and his words were thin and strained.

George saw him then, lying on the road on his back, pinned beneath a large boulder. A small dark stream of blood trickled from his mouth, bubbling as he breathed. George knew that his insides had to be badly smashed for that to happen, and he knew, too, that Joel Konda was dying.

"Tell Mrs. Konda not to sell," Joel said.

"I will, Mr. Konda."

"Promise me, you won't let her sell."

"I promise, but you can tell her yourself. You're goin' to be all right."

"I heard an explosion! What the hell happened here?" someone called out, and George looked around to see another one of Phelps' men arriving in a buckboard.

"Mr. Konda has been hurt," George said. "I need to take him home. Let me use your buckboard."

"He ain't none of my concern," the man in the buckboard said.

"I said I want to use your buckboard," George said more forcefully this time. He punctuated his request by pointing his pistol at the driver of the buckboard.

Joel spent a fitful night after they got him back to the Tilting K. The pain swept over his body in waves, carrying him almost to the threshold of his ability to endure it before finally backing away to allow him some relief. Trudy was holding his hand the entire time, and when the pain was at its sharpest he would squeeze Trudy's hand until her own pain was excruciating. But she never complained. Instead, she would return the squeeze, lending her husband some of her own strength.

The clock tolled off another hour.

"I will live until daybreak," Joel said, but his words were so quiet that Trudy had to put her ear right over his lips to hear them.

Joel stared at the window until the sky began to lighten. Finally the bright bars of early sunrise began streaming in.

"Open the window, please," Joel rasped. "I want to look at my ranch. I want to smell it, and hear it, one last time."

Fighting back the tears, Trudy pulled the

curtains all the way to one side, then raised the window. The silver light of early morning spilled in, projecting the lace shadows of a nearby fern onto the wall. Carried on the soft morning breeze was the faint scent of barnyard manure.

"Prop up my pillows," Joel said, and Trudy did as he asked.

Now Joel could see out, and he looked toward the corral and watched as two horses ran together, one of them biting the other playfully on the neck. The windmill whirred in the morning breeze. A rooster fluttered up to the corral fence, ruffled his feathers haughtily, then crowed proudly

"Go to the window," Joel said. "Let me use your eyes to look around."

Trudy got up and walked over to the window to look outside.

"Tell me what you see."

"I see the sun just coming up over the hills to the east," Trudy said. "The clouds are glowing gold and orange and red. And in the timbered notches of the hills, I can see a purple haze. On the rangeland rolling down from the higher country, there is an ocean of wild flowers of every hue and description. I see silver-leaf oak trees, flagging white as they flutter in the wind, and farther back, the dark green, almost blue, of the evergreen trees."

"You were a good wife to me, Trudy," Joel said. "Don't weep for me, girl. I've had as wonderful a life as any man could want."

When he said those words, Joel's voice had all the vitality and strength it had ever possessed. So vibrant were the words, that for a moment, Trudy allowed herself the irrational hope that he might recover. She turned to smile at him, but as she did so she saw his head slip down from the pillow and lie motionless.

"Joel?" she called. She moved quickly to his bed and saw that, though his eyes were open, the light had already left them. "Joel!" she said again, more quietly this time, because she knew he didn't hear her. Sadly, she put her hand to his face and closed his eyes. "And you were a wonderful husband, my darling," she said in a choked voice.

CHAPTER SIXTEEN

*Dobytown**
Nebraska Territory

Between the Cimarron in Kansas, and the
North Platte in the territory of Nebraska,
there was ample water and forage to allow the
cattle to hold up very well. Despite the fact
that half his drovers were women, Dick felt
that his outfit was the equal to any outfit that
had ever made a drive.

Though the relationship between the
others remained professional and platonic,
that wasn't the case between Ollie and Opal.
Older than the others, it soon became obvious that the attraction they felt for each
other went beyond the mere circumstance
of being thrown together. The situation was
helped along by the eager willingness of the
others to play Cupid. So caught up were

*Today known as Kearny, Nebraska.

they with Ollie and Opal's developing romance that few noticed the same thing was happening between Dick and Marline.

Through northern Kansas and southern Nebraska they often saw Indians following the herd from just out of range. At first they were worried about them, and for a while, Dick posted extra guards at night.

But it soon became obvious that the Indians had no intention of attacking. All they wanted was a few beeves, and they had a very ingenious method of accomplishing this. Always picking a part of the herd where there was the least chance of any encounter, the Indians would select a steer, then shoot him with a small arrow. The arrow would not penetrate deeply enough to kill, but the inflicted wound would weaken the steer to the point that it couldn't keep up with the herd. As the wounded animal fell back, the Indians would gather it in.

Dick knew what the Indians were doing, but he didn't know how to stop them short of a general war, and that he didn't want. As a result he decided to regard it as a means of paying toll for passing through their land, and he had no choice but to push the herd on through as quickly as he could, and that he did.

When they arrived at Dobytown, Dick

considered it lucky that they had only lost just over one hundred cows since leaving Texas. They had lost the most to the two stampedes — the one Coleman started, and the one they induced. They lost a few to the Indians, and the rest to various other causes. But by now they were three-fourths of the way through the drive. If they encountered no unexpected delays, they would easily reach Fort Sully before the first snowfall. They were feeling pretty satisfied with themselves, and Dick thought, rightfully so.

With the herd secure on the banks of the North Platte River, they drew lots to decide who would go into Dobytown first. Dick felt that the trip into town would be a respite his outfit had earned, and he had to admit that he was looking forward to it as much as any of them. He was glad, therefore, that his name had been one that came up in the first draw.

He didn't worry about Indians attacking those who stayed back to watch after the herd, because they were camped very near the Fort Kearney army post. Fort Kearney, established in 1848, was constructed by two companies of mounted Riflemen under the command of Lieutenant Colonel Ludwell Powell of the Missouri Mounted Volunteers. Built to protect the Oregon Trail, as well as the overland coach and mail routes to the West, the fort was manned all during the Civil War.

Just west of Fort Kearney on the north side of the North Platte River, enterprising civilians who wanted to capitalize on the military trade, as well as trade with the emigrants, fur traders, and boatmen, began building saloons and trading posts. The settlement soon became known as Dobytown.

By 1865, Dobytown consisted of half a dozen dirt streets, and some two hundred and fifty citizens. The two main streets were First Street, which ran roughly east and west, parallel with the North Platte River, and Central, which ran down from the north, connecting with First Street to form the letter "T." The outer edges of the town were dotted with small frame houses, barns, chicken coops, and privies. The more substantial commercial buildings competed for space closer to the middle of town.

Because there was no municipal government as such, no provisions had been made for street cleaners. As a result the streets were packed nearly solid with horse droppings. It not only made footing treacherous, it smelled, and the odor was particularly pungent after rain such as the one that had occurred early that morning.

It had already been announced that the Union Pacific Railroad would soon be coming through town, thus the future of Dobytown was assured. Indeed, some were already suggesting that the town should be renamed from the rather pejorative Dobytown, to a more respectable Kearney.

Most of the town's buildings were constructed of unfinished, whip-sawed lumber, though the hotel and one or two of the numerous saloons were painted. The saloons were decorated with rather garish signs, the work of a truly gifted sign painter whose skills would have brought him employment in any large city in the country. The gaudiest of all the signs was a large hand of cards depicting a royal flush in hearts. This was, appropriately enough, the Royal Flush Saloon.

Boardwalks had been laid in the center of town, with plank crossings at each corner. Though the boardwalk was also fouled with mud and offal, it did allow pedestrians some degree of mobility, and Dick Hodson and Marline Konda were making use of it as they visited the city.

Dick, Marline, Kitty, Opal, and Buck were the ones who had drawn lots to enjoy the town. Ron, Dooley, Ollie, Priscilla, and Anita were watching over the herd.

"Oh, Dick, look," Marline said, pointing to a building that advertised itself as the City Pig. "There's a restaurant. A real, live restaurant. Could we eat dinner there, please?"

"Are you sure you want to do that? We could probably eat four meals on the trail for what it would cost us to eat one meal in there."

"Oh, don't be such a penny pincher," Marline teased. "It's not going to break us to have a meal in a real restaurant. If I weren't with you, you would probably spend that much money in the saloon."

Dick smiled, then nodded. "You're right, I probably would. Kitty is a good cook, but it would be nice to eat a meal while sitting at a table. All right, just this once."

"Oh, thank you!" Marline said, her eyes shining with delight at the prospect.

They were greeted by a pleasant-faced, middle-aged woman when they stepped inside the establishment. "Hello, folks, I don't think I've ever seen you in here before. Did you just arrive at Fort Kearney?"

"No, ma'am," Dick answered. "We're from Texas, pushing a herd of cattle up to the Dakota Territory."

"My, you come all the way from Texas driving a herd of cattle?" the woman said.

"You've come a long way."

"Yes, ma'am, it is a long way."

"Well, what can I fix for you nice folks? I have roast pork, fried chicken, chicken and dumplings, and a nice beef stew."

"I'll have the roast pork," Dick ordered.

"Fried chicken," Marline said.

"I'll have that too," Dick said.

"Instead of the roast pork?"

Dick smiled. "No, ma'am. With the roast pork."

The woman laughed. "Your husband is quite an eater, honey," she said to Marline. "I can see you're going to have a lifetime of cooking in front of you."

"Oh, he isn't —" Marline started, but Dick interrupted her.

"Always this hungry," he concluded, reaching over to let his fingers rest lightly on Marline's hand. Marline looked at him questioningly. "It's just that we've been on the trail for a while."

"Well, if you folks are that hungry, I'd better get busy in the kitchen," the woman said as she walked away.

"Why did you stop me from telling her that you aren't my husband?" Marline asked.

"I don't know," Dick answered. He smiled at her warmly. "I guess the idea of her thinking that just appealed to me."

Across the street from the restaurant in the Royal Flush Saloon, Buck Corbin pushed through the batwing doors, then stopped just inside to take a look around. In keeping with the promise of the sign, the Royal Flush was a well-appointed saloon, with a long mahogany bar that stretched down the left side of the room. The bar was decorated with a shining brass foot rail, interspersed with bronze rings placed about four feet apart on the customers' side, from which hung towels for their use. Behind the bar was a long shelf filled with bottles of various shapes, sizes, and hues. The bottles repeated themselves in the mirror behind the shelf.

On the wall to the rear of the saloon hung an oversized painting, the subject of which was a voluptuous nude woman. She was lying on a red couch receiving a note from a small, nude cherub who stood beside her.

Two wood-burning stoves, cold now, but still smelling of last winter's efforts, sat in the middle of the room, surrounded by tables and chairs. The saloon was large enough to accommodate forty or fifty customers, though at the moment there were no more than ten people present, most of whom were standing at the bar.

On the opposite wall from the bar was a piano. It was badly out of tune, a fact that was very evident as a cigar-smoking, derby-hatted, garter-sleeved pianist banged away at the keys, half of which were missing their ivory coverings. Despite the cacophonous accompaniment, two bar girls were singing the Civil War ballad "Lorena," and doing a surprisingly good job of it.

Buck stepped up to the bar.

"What'll it be?" the bartender asked.

"I'll have a beer," Buck said.

"Sonny, you're a little young to be drinking with the menfolk, aren't you?" someone asked from the far end of the bar. "Don't your mama have a sugartit for you to suck on?"

Buck glanced down at his heckler, an average-sized man whose pockmarked face was accented by a pair of beady eyes, a sweeping mustache, and a purple scar on his left cheek. Buck stared at him for a long moment before he turned his attention back to the bartender, who was wiping out a beer mug to fill his order.

"Did you hear what I asked you, boy?" the scar-faced man asked, obviously miffed that Buck had turned away from him. "I asked if your mama didn't have a sugartit for you to suck on?" He cackled, and a few of the men who were close by laughed nervously as well. Most stared into their drinks, trying to avoid any entanglement in what was obviously the baiting of an innocent stranger.

"I heard what you said," Buck finally said.

"Them sugartits sure is sweet, ain't they?" the scar-faced man asked. "But then, pup that you are, I'll just bet your mama's titties are sweeter. That right, boy? Your mama got some real sweet little titties?"

"Mr. Clay, this boy ain't done nothin' no more'n come in here for a drink," the bartender said as he began drawing Buck's beer. "There ain't no need for you to torment him so. Why don't you leave him alone?"

Clay glared at the bartender "Are you wantin' a part of this, barkeep?" he asked with a snarl.

"No . . . no sir," the barkeep stuttered, backing away, quickly. "I was just . . ." Whatever he was "just" was left unsaid, as he decided the quicker he could withdraw from this, the better he would be.

"You were just what?" Clay asked the bartender.

"Nothin', Mr. Clay. Not a thing."

"I didn't think you wanted any of this." Clay nodded toward Buck. "If this boy thinks he's old enough to come into a man's bar and drink with the men, then he's old enough to look out for his ownself." He turned his attention back to Buck. "Ain't that right, boy? So, how about it? Are you old enough?"

"Well, I don't know," Buck replied. Turning now to face Clay, he stared at him through unblinking eyes. "Just how old does a person have to be to kill a man?" Buck asked.

Clay blinked in surprise. "To kill a man? Is that what you said?"

Buck stared at him without a blink or twitch. It was obvious that he wasn't in the least bit afraid. "Yes, that's exactly what I said."

Clay cleared his throat. He was puzzled by this boy's unusual behavior. Why wasn't the boy afraid of him? "You think you're old enough to kill a man?" he asked.

"You aren't much of a man, so I reckon I'm old enough to kill you," Buck said.

Buck's words elicited a gasp of surprise from everyone who was close enough to hear them. Addison Clay was more than surprised, he was thunderstruck. "What?" Clay thundered.

"Boy!" the bartender said quickly, as he put the mug of beer in front of Buck. "Don't you know who this is? This here is Addison Clay."

"Addison Clay," Buck repeated. "Is that a name I should know?"

"He's kilt more'n twenty men," the bartender said nervously.

"He's a real killer, is he?" Buck asked, as he reached for his beer with his left hand. "He doesn't look like much to me."

Addison Clay was confused and frustrated. It was his way to feed on the fear that his name and his reputation engendered in people. But for some reason, this boy was denying him that. Clearly, the boy didn't know enough to be frightened.

"Boy, seein' as you don't know who I am, I'm goin' to let you off easy this time," Clay said.

"Thanks."

Clay chuckled. "I said I was goin' to let you off easy, I didn't say I was goin' to let you off for nothin'. Now, what I want you to do is slide that beer on down to me."

"Now why would I want to do something like that?"

"Let's say it would be your way of makin' it up to me."

Buck chuckled, then blew the head off the beer. "Right," he said sarcastically.

Addison Clay realized that in the eyes of

the others in here, the boy was getting the upper hand. He had to reestablish control, and quickly.

"Touch your lips to that mug, boy, and you're a dead man," Clay said sharply, moving his hand into position just over his pistol.

These were killing words, and when Clay spoke them, all other conversation in the saloon came to a halt. The piano player stopped playing, and the music broke off awkwardly in a few, ragged, uneven, and incomplete bars. The girls who had been singing stopped as well and looked on in openmouthed awe as the saloon grew deathly silent. The loudest sound in the room was the steady ticking of the old Terry clock that was measuring time from the wall next to the painting.

"I beg your pardon?" Buck replied.

Very deliberately, Clay drew his pistol and pointed it at Buck, then cocked it. When the sear engaged the cylinder it made a deadly sound, a sound that no one who heard it would ever forget, like the warning of a rattlesnake.

"You heard me. I said I would kill you if you touch your lips to that beer."

Buck flashed an icy smile as he brought the mug up to his lips. Then, before anyone realized what he was doing, Buck let go of the mug. Time seemed to be standing still, for the beer mug just hung in midair for an instant as Buck fell backward.

It was as if Buck had known the exact moment Clay would pull the trigger, because as the gunman fired, his bullet crashed through the mug, sending a shower of beer and shards of glass flying in all directions.

Addison Clay's attention had been riveted on the beer mug, which was exactly what Buck had wanted to happen. That diversion allowed Buck to fall to the floor, taking him out of the line of fire. As Buck was falling, he pulled his own pistol, then lying his back on the barroom floor, he fired, hitting Clay in the shoulder.

"You little son of a bitch!" Clay shouted, enraged that he had been tricked. Clay shifted his attention from the shattered beer mug to Buck. He fired a second time, but again anticipating it, Buck rolled quickly to his right. Clay's second bullet passed harmlessly by, punching a hole in the floor where Buck had been but a second earlier.

Buck fired a second time, this time hitting Clay where his neck joined his chin. The bullet exited the back of Clay's head, spraying a little mist of blood, brain matter, and bone fragments as it did. The pistol slipped out of Clay's hand, and Buck's would-be killer tumbled backward. Addison Clay was dead before his body even hit the floor.

The four discharges formed a heavy cloud that drifted to the ceiling then spread out to cover the entire saloon. The place reeked with the stench of cordite.

"Did you see that?" someone asked in a stunned voice.

"I never thought I'd live to see the day someone could beat Addison Clay."

"Well, if you ask me, the son of a bitch needed killin'," another said. "If there was ever anyone who needed killin', it was Addison Clay."

Buck got up from the floor, dusted off the seat of his pants, then stepped back up to the bar.

"I'll trouble you for another beer, if you don't mind," he said calmly.

"Yes, sir!" the bartender replied, awed by the young man's calmness.

Dick was just about to start on a piece of apple pie when Kitty and Opal came into the restaurant. Seeing Dick and Marline, they hurried over to the table, their faces etched with worry.

"Hello, ladies, won't you join us?" Dick invited.

"Dick, we have a problem. Buck is in jail," Kitty said without any greeting.

"What? Why? What did he do?"

"He killed someone," Opal said.

"My God, are you serious?"

"Everyone says it was in self-defense," Kitty said quickly. "Opal and I heard them talking about it in the general store."

"Well, I don't understand. If it's self-defense and they have witnesses, why would they have him in jail?" Marline asked.

"I don't know the answer to that. We didn't ask any questions," Opal replied. "As soon as we heard about it, we came to find you two."

"Maybe we had better go see what's going on," Dick suggested, leaving enough money on the table to pay for his and Marline's meal.

The town constable for Dobyville was overweight to the point of obesity. Sitting at his desk, eating a sweet roll, and reading a newspaper, he began chuckling just as Dick, Marline, Kitty, and Opal came into his office.

"Listen to this," he said, looking up at them. He read from the paper. "A man went to the bank with his wife. 'I would like to cash her in, please,' he says to the teller. 'Cash her in for what?' the teller responds. 'Well, she's forty,' the man says. 'I would like to exchange her for two twenty-year-olds.' " Laughing out loud, the constable hit the top of his desk with the palm of his hand. "If that ain't a rip-snorter, though." He pushed the paper to one side. "All right, now, what can I do for you folks?"

"Constable, my name is Dick Hodson."

"And these ladies are?" the constable asked, looking at them through porcine eyes.

"With me," Dick replied without introducing them. "We're driving a herd of cows through here, and I think you may have one of our men in your jail. Do you have a prisoner here named Buck Corbin?" Dick asked.

"I reckon I do."

"Why are you holding him?"

"We're holding him, Mr. Hodson, because he killed a man," the constable said.

"But it was self-defense," Kitty said.

The constable looked pointedly at Kitty. "Well, now, little lady, how do you know that? Were you there?"

"No, but I heard it was self-defense."

"Uh-huh. Well, I heard that too, but this

whole thing seems a little fishy to me."

"How so?" Dick asked.

"I've know'd Addison Clay for the better part of a year now. I'm not callin' him my friend, don't get me wrong about that. But I know how good he was with a gun. He was fast, he could shoot straight, and he could kill a man with no more thought than it would take to step on a cockroach. Despite all that, this boy not only killed Clay, they say he wasn't even afraid of him. So I intend to hold young Buck Corbin for trial, just to make sure everything is done right."

"How long will a trial take?" Dick asked.

"Oh, if all the witnesses say the same thing — that it was self-defense — I don't reckon the trial will last more'n a few minutes," the constable said.

Dick sighed, and smiled, broadly. "That's good. I was afraid we might be tied up here for a while."

"We? What do you mean we?"

"I told you, Buck Corbin is part of our outfit. Anything that affects him, affects us. How soon will you hold the trial?"

"We'll hold it next time the circuit judge comes through."

"When is that?" Dick asked.

"Let me see," the constable said lifting the page on the calendar. "Looks like he'll be here in about three more weeks."

"Three weeks? Are you telling me Buck has to stay in your jail for three more weeks? What about bail? Can't we pay his bail and get him out of jail until the trial?"

"The judge has to set bail," the constable said. "And bein' as he ain't here, there ain't no bail. But you won't be needin' bail anyhow. Soon as the judge holds his trial the boy will more'n likely be set free. Hell, the way folks around here felt about Addison Clay, they'll probably be wantin' to give your friend a medal."

"May we visit him?" Kitty asked.

"Sure, be my guest. He's back there," the constable said with a wave of his hand. "Go on back and visit for as long as you like."

Kitty, Opal, Marline, and Dick went through the door the constable had pointed out. Beyond the door was another room, perhaps even a little larger than the front office. This room was divided into four cells, with two cells on each side. The right front cell was occupied by a sleeping prisoner. Two were empty, and Buck was in the left rear cell, sitting on the hard bunk. His knees were drawn up before him, and his arms were wrapped around his legs. He looked up and smiled wanly as Dick and the others approached.

"Hi, Buck," Dick greeted.

"Hi, ya'll," Buck replied. "Guess I sort of spoiled our trip to town, didn't I? But the son of a bitch left me no choice. It was either kill him, or get killed. Sorry about the language, ladies," he added.

"Everyone is saying it was self-defense," Kitty said. "And the constable just told us you'll be set free."

"I sort of figured they would see it my way," Buck said, though the relief in his voice was evident. "At least, I hoped they would. There were some other folks there, and they all saw what happened."

"There is a problem, though," Dick said. "The constable plans to keep you in jail until the trial, and that's not for another three weeks."

"That's no good. Dick, you can't wait three weeks," Buck said. "If you hang around here that long, you could get caught in the first winter's snow."

"I know," Dick said. "I'm glad you can see that. I'm glad you understand."

"Understand what?" Marline asked. "Dick, what are you talking about? You aren't planning on leaving him here, are you?"

"I've got no choice," Dick said. "We have to keep moving. If we are still on the trail when that first winter storm hits, we could lose from half to three-fourths of our herd. Maybe more."

"Dick, please," Marline begged. "What if you were the one sitting in that cell? Do you think we'd leave you?"

"I would hope that you would," Dick said.

"Dick's right. You have to leave me here," Buck said. Then he smiled at Kitty. "Unless you decide to bake me a cake with a file inside," he teased.

"Buck, what kind of view do you have through that back window?" Kitty asked.

"View?" Buck replied, surprised by the question. "Why, I don't know, I haven't looked."

"Take a look back there, will you?"

Buck walked back to the rear of his cell. The window was set near the top of the wall, and Buck was so short he had to move the bunk over and stand on it in order to see through the bars.

"As far as I can tell, there's nothin' back here but the alley," Buck said.

"No houses or buildings?"

"None that I can see. Why are you so interested in the view?"

"No particular reason. I was just curious, that's all."

"Kitty, you are a smart woman," Buck

said. "But you do have some peculiar ways about you."

After leaving the jail, they started toward the stable where they had put up their horses for the day.

"Damn, I hate leaving him there," Dick said.

"You don't have to."

Dick sighed. "Yes, we do. I've explained that."

"We can break him out."

"How?"

"Not how, why?" Opal said. "I mean, if he breaks jail, won't that just make matters worse? Even the constable believes it was self-defense. If he waits until the trial, he'll be found innocent. But if we do this, he'll be guilty of breaking out of jail."

"Once we get him away from Dobytown, the town constable will have no authority over him. And once we get him out of Nebraska, he can't be brought back into the territory except by extradition, which means a federal extradition. The folks here aren't going to go to all the trouble to extradite someone that everyone, even the constable, knows is innocent. All we have to do is get him away from here, and he'll be home free."

"All right, that makes sense to me," Dick

said. "Kitty, if you have some idea as to how we can get him out, I say let's do it. I don't want to leave him here anymore than anyone else does."

Chapter Seventeen

When Dick, Marline, Kitty, and Opal returned to the place where they had left the herd, Dick gave them the news about Buck.

"I'm sorry to have to tell you this, but that means you folks won't be able to go to town," he said. "We are going to have to get the herd as far away from this place as we can by nightfall," he said. "The farther away we are, the less the likelihood they'll come after us."

"Wait a minute, if Buck is the one who shot the man, and if he is already in jail, why would they be coming after us?" Ron asked.

"Because we're going to break Buck out of jail," Dick said. "Or rather, Kitty is."

"Kitty is?"

"With our help," Dick added. He looked at Kitty. "So, what will you need from us?" he asked, rubbing his hands together.

"First thing I'll need is the team of mules," Kitty said. "So that means we'll have to hitch a couple of horses to the chuck wagon, and someone else will have to drive it on ahead," Kitty said.

"I'll drive the wagon," Opal volunteered.

"What are you going to do with the mules?" Dick asked. "Do you think they can pull out one of those bars?"

"Oh! I hope none of the bars come out," Kitty replied. "If they do, we'll lose leverage," Kitty said.

"Wait a minute, I think I'm beginning to see the picture here," Dooley said. "Is the barred window at the top of the wall?"

"Yes, at the very top," Kitty answered.

Dooley laughed. "You are going to apply the Archimedes principle, aren't you?"

"That's it," Kitty replied, smiling that Dooley had understood at once what she had in mind.

"The Archimedes principle? What is an Archimedes? Will someone please tell me what is going on?" Dick asked.

"Archimedes isn't a what, he's a who," Dooley explained. "Archimedes was a mathematician who lived in Greece a long time ago. He once said, 'Give me a lever long enough, and a place to stand, and I can move the world.' "

Dick and the others looked at each other in confusion.

Dooley laughed. "You don't get it, do you?"

"No," Dick admitted.

"It's mechanical advantage," Kitty explained. "The window is at the top of the brick wall, and the bars are imbedded in the wall. Because of that, the wall can be considered a lever."

"Which means, all we have to do is apply enough pulling force to those bars, and the entire wall will come tumbling down," Dooley added.

"Just like Joshua blowing his horn," Kitty said with a laugh.

"So, we have Joshua, too, now, do we? Well, with people like Archimedes and Joshua on our side, how can we possibly fail?" Marline teased.

The others laughed.

"I'll be damned," Dick said. "Maybe I'm as crazy as you two, but I think I'm beginning to see what you are talking about." He looked at Kitty. "Do you really think the window is high enough? Will it give you enough leverage?"

"If the mules are strong enough, it just might work," Kitty replied.

Although Dick had furnished the wagon, it was Ron Sietz who supplied the mules. Dick turned to him.

"What about it, Ron? Do you think your mules are up to it?"

"Listen, I've seen those two pull stumps out of the ground," Ron said proudly. "What is it that fella Archimedes said? Give him a lever long enough, and a place to stand, and he would move the world? Well, my mules can't move the world, but if you give 'em a place to stand, they'll damn sure pull that wall down for you."

It was just after midnight when Dick, Dooley, Ron, and Kitty rode into town. The others were with the herd, now some fifteen miles farther north.

Ron was leading the two mules while Dick led Buck's horse, already saddled and ready to go. In the entire town, only two lights could be seen. A very dim light, probably a candle, flickered from the back of one of the houses, while upstairs at the Royal Flush Saloon, a lantern burned brightly.

Through the open window of one of the houses, they could hear snoring. A baby was crying at another house while, from the alley, came the yap of a dog who was both protective and curious.

"It's back here," Dick whispered, leading them off the street and up the alley. Because the alley was much less traveled than the street, it was still covered with grass. That was to their advantage, for the grass cushioned the sound of falling hoofbeats. The four rode up the alley until they came to the back wall of the jail. Once there, Dick climbed up onto the back of his horse and, standing on the saddle, looked inside. He found himself staring into a pitch black maw.

"Buck! Buck, are you in there?" Dick called in a hoarse whisper.

"Yeah, I'm here."

"Where's the constable?" Dick hissed.

"Far as I know, he's up front, sound asleep," Buck replied.

"Stand back away from the wall," Dick said. Dooley passed a couple of ropes up to Dick, then Dick looped them around the bars then sent the ends back down. Ron hitched the team, then looked at Dick.

"Do it," Dick ordered.

At Dick's command, Ron slapped the reins against the backs of the two mules.

"Come on, Harry, come on, Frank," Ron called softly, urging the team on.

The mules strained into the harness, the ropes tightened, and the bars began to creak.

"Come on, boys, you can do it!" Ron said, exhorting his mules.

Dick, Kitty, and Dooley helped Ron urge the mules on as they pulled and strained. One of them pulled so hard he lost his footing and slipped down on one knee, but recovered quickly.

A faint, grinding sound came from the back wall of the jail.

"It's working!" Kitty said. "I can hear it!"

Dooley grabbed one of the ropes and began pulling, helping the mules. Dick took the other rope. The mules, Dooley, and Dick pulled as hard as they could. Then, without any further warning, three-fourths of the back wall suddenly toppled down, the bricks tumbling across each other as a cloud of dust rose into the midnight air.

A half-dozen dogs then began to bark.

"What the hell was that?" someone shouted from one of the darkened houses.

Here and there, lanterns and candles were lit, and little bubbles of light began to appear.

"Ed, what is it? What's going on out there?" a woman's voice called from within the darkness of one of the houses.

"Come on, Buck, get out of there," Dick hissed.

Coughing and waving his hand in front of his face to dispel the brick and mortar dust, Buck walked through the gap in the wall, climbed over the pile of bricks, then mounted the horse Dick had brought for him. At the same time, Ron was taking the harness off the team of mules, getting them ready to run as well.

"Let's go!" Dick shouted, and the five young Texans galloped out of town while shouts of surprise and confusion erupted behind them.

"Yahoo!" Buck shouted at the top of his lungs. "That was the most fun I've had in my whole life!"

Fort Kearney, Nebraska

Although no more than ten people had been in the saloon when Buck shot Addison Clay, within two days after he broke out of jail there were at least twenty who were making the claim that they had "seen it all." The story spread through town, then spilled over into nearby Fort Kearney.

News that Addison Clay was dead was welcomed by the authorities at the post, because at least two of Addison Clay's earlier victims had been soldiers. Captain Marcus Cavanaugh could remember the day he arrived at Kearney as a transfer from Fort Sully, Dakota Territory. As he climbed

263

down from the stage he saw the two young soldiers lying dead on the boardwalk in front of the Royal Flush Saloon. Evidently the shooting had just occurred, for people were hurrying to the scene from all over town.

Because Cavanaugh was in uniform, the town constable assumed he had come for the bodies. He hadn't of course — he had only just arrived — but he accepted the responsibility, renting a wagon from the livery to take the two soldiers out to the fort. Once there, he turned them over to the provost marshal.

Although the constable assured the provost marshal that the two young men died in a "fair fight with Addison Clay," Cavanaugh was interested enough in what had happened to conduct his own investigation. He learned that the two privates had been sharing a table with a bar girl named Mable. When Clay demanded that Mable leave them and sit with him, she refused, and Clay threatened her. The soldiers, unaware of Clay's deadly reputation, came to her defense. One word led to another until pistols were pulled, and bullets were fired. When the smoke rolled away, the two young men in Army Blue lay dead on the boardwalk in front of the saloon.

When word had reached the fort that Addison Clay had been killed by someone who was little more than a boy, there were no tears shed. And when the soldiers learned that the boy had escaped by having his friends come into town in the middle of the night and pull down the back wall of the jailhouse, the men, several of whom had spent a night or two in the jail themselves for public drunkenness, celebrated that fact and drank toasts to the escapee.

"It was a group of young Texans," Colonel Patterson told Cavanaugh when he asked about it. "Men and women, from what I hear. Or, maybe I should say boys and girls, because I'm told they were all kids, no more than seventeen or eighteen. According to the constable, the only one over the age of twenty was the trailboss. Seems they were driving a herd of cattle through here. Though where they were going with them, I have no idea."

"Damn!" Cavanaugh said, hitting his fist into his hand. "I know where they are going."

"Where?"

"They're going to Fort Sully."

"What makes you think that?"

"Because I told him that if he could get a herd up to Fort Sully, the army would pay forty dollars a head for every cow delivered."

"You told who?"

"Dick Hodson."

"You think this is the same person?" Colonel Patterson asked.

"I'm afraid it is. With your permission, sir, I'll ride into town and find out. If it is the same person, I need to get word to him before he gets any farther. Captain Fitzhugh, who replaced me at Fort Sully, has made his own arrangements. I wouldn't want Hodson to get all the way up there with his herd, and then not have a market."

"Permission granted," Colonel Patterson said.

"I can't exactly remember his name," the constable responded to Cavanaugh's question. "I only met him that once. He gave me his name, but I don't recall it."

"What did he look like?"

"Oh, he was a nice enough lookin' young fella," the constable said. "Had that sort of lean, leathery Texas look about him. I'd make him to be about five feet ten or so, good features. As I recall, he walked with a limp."

"A limp you say?"

"Yes. Seemed like it didn't slow him down

all that much, but you could tell he was bad hurt in the leg at one time or another. I figure it must've been the war. He looked old enough to have been a part of it."

"If I had any doubts as to who it was before, those doubts are gone now. It's Dick Hodson, all right," Cavanaugh said.

"Hodson!" the constable said, snapping his fingers. "Yes, that's it. I knew it would come to me. The fella's name was Dick Hodson."

Captain Cavanaugh smiled. "You're sure now," he said.

"I'm positive. I never forget a name, though I can't quite recollect the name of the girl that was with him. Why are you so interested, anyway?"

"That herd he is driving? He's taking it to Fort Sully to sell to the army."

"Fort Sully? Where's that?"

"It's in Dakota Territory."

The constable whistled. "That's a long way off, ain't it?"

"Yes."

"He'll be lucky if he gets those cows up there before winter sets in."

"The sad thing is, when he gets there with his herd, he'll have no market," Captain Cavanaugh said. "The army has already made other arrangements."

"Is that a fact?" The constable chuckled. "Well I tell you what, Captain, I just can't get all worked up over Mr. Hodson's problems. I mean, not after what he done to my jail and all. Don't know why it should bother you none, either."

"It bothers me because I was the one who made the initial offer to him. He's driving those cattle some fifteen hundred miles, and when he gets there it will all be for nothing."

"Neither the United States Government nor the Territory of Nebraska is goin' to send anyone after 'em. And that's too bad, 'cause I'd sure like to see 'em brought back here so I could make 'em pay for the damage they done to my jail."

Fort Sully, Dakota Territory

The last three weeks of the drive were unexpectedly easy. As they were following the Missouri River north by northwest, there was never a shortage of water. Because deer and antelope used the river for water, there was also an ample supply of game. As a result, Kitty outdid herself with the dishes she prepared, and some of the girls even complained that they were eating so well that they were getting fat.

When Dick perceived that they were getting close to the military reservation, he began sending scouts ahead to look for it. It surprised no one when Anita came back to report that she had found it.

"Yahoo! We made it!" Ron said. "I don't know about the rest of you but I, for one, will be glad to get rid of these dumb beasts."

"Oh, you don't mean that, Ron," Priscilla teased. "I've seen the way you act around them. Why, you've made pets of every one of them."

The others laughed, even as they noticed that Ron and Priscilla were beginning to spend more time with each other. It was not just a working association — it was obviously developing into a more personal relationship.

Other working teams had begun to blossom into personal alliances as well. Anita and Buck seemed to be a natural pair. Both were excellent riders, and of all the women, Anita was most adept at roping, shooting, and scouting. And Buck had already proven himself to be deadly expert with a pistol.

Ollie and Opal seemed drawn together as well. It might have been because both considered themselves outsiders, and neither had any personal investment in the drive —

none of the cows were theirs. It might also have been because both were leaving behind situations that they wanted to get away from, for in a very real sense, Opal's time as a prostitute had made her every bit as much a prisoner as Ollie's time in Elmyra.

Dooley and Kitty seemed a natural pair. Both were extremely intelligent and exceptionally well read. Their relationship began with a shared love for books, and even before anyone else began pairing off, Dooley and Kitty would often sit apart from the others, discussing authors and philosophies of life.

The final pairing to show itself was Dick and Marline. Dick was attracted to Marline from the very beginning, though he felt it would be hazardous to good order for him to show it. On the other hand, Marline's secret devotion for Dick was no secret from her friends. She had developed a crush on him back when she was twelve years old, when Dick and her brother were the best of friends. That adolescent crush had long ago blossomed into love.

With all other relationships now out in the open, Dick no longer felt quite as constrained in expressing his desire to spend time with Marline, and when he asked her if she would ride to the fort with him to make the arrangements to drop off the herd and pick up the money, no one was surprised.

"Money? Well, now, that word has a rather nice ring to it, don't you think?" Marline replied. "Yes, I'll be happy to ride with you."

"Ron, while we're gone, why don't you and the others see what you can do toward getting a final count?" Dick asked. "If we are going to be paid, we need to know how much we are being paid for."

"We'll do it," Ron promised.

"There, I see it," Marline said about an hour later. Dick looked in the direction in which Marline had pointed. There, perched on the end of a high bluff that protruded over the Missouri River, was the fort. Constructed of log palisades, there were two projecting blockhouses on corners opposite each other from which, Dick realized, the guards not only had a view of the river approach and the surrounding countryside, but could also cover by riflefire the outside walls of the fort itself. An American flag fluttered from a pole atop the nearer blockhouse.

"Well, this is it. This is what we came for. What do you say we go take care of our business?" Dick suggested.

Marline ran her hand through her hair. "Lord, after so many months on the trail, what I must look like," she complained.

Dick laughed. "Well, you didn't care what you looked like as long as you were with us, but get around a bunch of Yankee soldier-boys and you want to look your best. Damned if I'm not jealous," Dick quipped.

"What?" Marline gasped. "Why, Dick Hodson, how could you think such a thing?"

Dick laughed. "I was just teasing," he said. "Besides, you look beautiful. You always look beautiful."

Marline didn't think she could actually do so now, not after months on the trail, but she found herself blushing at Dick's words.

"Why, I . . . I thank you for that," she stammered.

When Dick realized how touched she really was by his compliment, it was his time to be embarrassed.

Because they had stumbled upon an awkward moment in their relationship, they didn't speak again as they rode up to the front gate of the fort. The gate was opened, but it was manned by two military guards. One of them stepped forward and brought his rifle up to port arms.

"Halt! Who goes there?" the guard challenged.

"I'm Dick Hodson. This is Miss Marline Konda. We are here on army business," Dick replied. "We would like to speak with Captain Marcus Cavanaugh."

"Captain Cavanaugh?" the guard asked. "I ain't never heard of no Captain Cavanaugh." He looked over at the other guard. "Porter, do you know a Captain Cavanaugh?"

The other guard started to shake his head no, then he stopped. "Wait a minute, yeah, I think I do remember him. He commanded B Troop. But he left quite a while ago."

Dick felt a twinge of uneasiness. "Are you telling me Captain Cavanaugh isn't here?"

"That's what we're telling you, mister," the guard said.

Dick stroked his chin for a moment, then he remembered Lieutenant Kirby.

"What about Lieutenant Kirby? Is he still here?"

"Kirby? Yeah, he's still here."

"Then I would like to see him."

"Porter, go get Kirby. Tell him he has a visitor at the gate."

While Porter was gone, Dick dismounted and led his horse over to the precipice, standing there for a moment staring down at the river. Marline walked up beside him.

"Dick, is everything all right?" she asked.

"I wish I could say yes, but I don't know," Dick admitted. "I have an awfully uneasy feeling about all this."

"Oh, please, God, we didn't come all this way not to be able to sell our cows," Marline said quietly, expressing the prayer that Dick felt as well.

"Mister, here's Lieutenant Kirby," the guard called a few moments later.

"Something I can do for you, Mister . . ." Kirby started, then recognizing Dick, he smiled and extended his hand. "Why, if it isn't Mr. Hodson," he said. "It's good seeing you again. What are you doing up in this neck of the woods?"

"What am I doing up here? I brought the cattle."

Kirby looked confused. "The cattle? What cattle?"

"The cattle Cavanaugh asked me to bring. Don't you remember? We were eating dinner when . . ." Dick paused in mid-sentence as he realized that Kirby hadn't been present during that dinner. Unless Cavanaugh had mentioned it to him, Kirby would have no way of knowing about the cattle.

"You don't know what I'm talking about, do you? You don't know anything about the cattle."

"No, sir, I'm afraid not," Kirby answered in a voice that showed his obvious confusion.

Dick sighed. "I've got three thousand head of cattle we drove up from Texas," he said. "They're waiting about two miles downriver from here. I brought them up here because Cavanaugh promised that the army would pay forty dollars per head for them."

Kirby shook his head in dismay. "Oh . . . uh, I think maybe you'd better talk to Colonel May," he suggested.

"Yes, I think I'd better," Dick agreed.

A bullet-scarred Confederate flag was on the wall of Colonel May's office. When Colonel May saw Dick looking at it, he chuckled. "That flag belonged to the Fifth Mississippi Infantry," he said. "My command took it away from them at the Battle of Pittsburgh Landing."

"Shiloh was a hard-fought battle, all right," Dick said.

"You call it Shiloh? Then you were on the other side." It was a statement, not a question.

"Yes, sir," Dick replied.

Colonel May took a cigar from his humidor. Holding it up, he glanced toward Marline.

"Will it offend you if we smoke, my dear?" he asked.

"No, sir, not at all," Marline replied.

Colonel May took out a second cigar and offered it to Dick. Dick accepted with thanks, then bit the end off while Colonel May prepared his own in a like fashion. From the same match, Colonel May lit both Dick's cigar and his own. Not until their heads were wreathed in smoke did the commander speak again.

"So as I understand it, you brought three thousand head of cattle all the way up from Texas?"

"Yes, sir."

"And Captain Cavanaugh told you that the army would buy your herd?"

"Yes, sir, at forty dollars a head."

"Well, at the time Cavanaugh told you that, he was acting in good faith," May said. "For in his initial orders, he was told to purchase as many head of cattle as he could find. But when other arrangements were made, contravening orders were issued. Unfortunately Captain Cavanaugh didn't find out about those new orders until it was too late to tell you."

"Colonel, are you saying you can't use these cattle in any way, shape, or form?"

"I'm afraid not, Mr. Hodson. I can only

spend what money the government gives me, and I simply don't have enough money to buy your herd. Not at forty dollars a head, not even at ten dollars a head."

"Oh, Dick, what are we going to do?" Marline asked, her voice betraying the fact that she was on the verge of tears.

"You could try the railroad," Colonel May suggested.

"What railroad?" Dick asked. "There is no railroad out here."

"No, but there soon will be," Colonel May said. "I'm sure you've heard of the great transcontinental railroad that is being built. They're somewhere down in Nebraska right now, with an army of track layers as big as any army that took to the field during the late war. When you have that many men, they have to eat. Right now the buffalo hunters are barely able to keep up with the demand."

"What are they paying?" Dick asked.

"Six cents a pound, on the hoof."

"Six cents a pound?" Dick replied excitedly. "Why, that's more than the army was going to give us! Six cents a pound will run to nearly fifty dollars per head."

Colonel May shook his head no. "I'm afraid not," he said. "They are paying six cents a pound against an average of five hundred pounds per animal."

"What?" Dick replied. "Why, even our scrawniest cows weigh more than that."

"That's their price," Colonel May said. "It's your choice whether or not you take it."

Dick snorted what may have been a laugh. "Choice? What choice? It's either take their offer, turn them loose, or drive them back. Where is the choice in that?"

CHAPTER EIGHTEEN

End of Track

Samuel Reed was a busy man. As construction chief for the Union Pacific Railroad, it was his job to push the tracks across western America. The men he employed to do this task consisted of Civil War veterans from both the North and the South, freed slaves, Irish and German immigrants, men who had a taste for adventure, and men who were fleeing their past.

On average, the railroad would advance from two to five miles per day. On its western transit the men filled ravines, built huge trestles across rivers and valleys, and were already punching holes through mountains in anticipation of the track to come.

Outside Sam Reed's office, which was in fact a specially constructed railcar, the men scurried about with enough activity and energy to put an ant colony to shame.

First to be laid down would be the cross-ties, dropped into a place precisely marked out by the section chief. As soon as one cross-tie would go down, the men who carried it up would peel around and go back to get another one, even as the two men behind them were putting their own tie into place.

Next would be the rails. Flatcars brought the rails to within half a mile of the end of track, where the rails were loaded onto carts. The horse-drawn cart would then move quickly up to the front with its load. When they were as close as they could go, two men would seize the end of a rail and start forward. As they snaked the rail from the cart, others would join by twos until the rail was clear. As soon as the rail was clear of the cart, the men would start forward at a run. At a barked, rhythmic command, the rail would be dropped into place. The entire procedure was repeated every thirty seconds of daylight so that the railroad moved inexorably forward.

Behind the flatcars came the triple-decker cars which were, in effect, rolling bunkhouses. Behind them came the kitchen and dining car.

It was the kitchen and dining car that had

kept Emil Sawyer occupied, supplying meat for the kitchen.

Until now.

Sawyer had just been told by Sam Reed that the UP wouldn't be buying any more buffalo for a while.

"What do you mean you don't want any more?" Sawyer asked in a blustery, belligerent voice.

"I mean we have no need of it now," Reed said. He signed off on two survey reports and gave them back to the surveyors who had brought them to him. "Haven't you noticed? We've just bought an entire herd of cattle now."

"Why would you do that?" Sawyer asked.

"By not butchering the meat until we actually need it, we can keep it much fresher. It's healthier, and the men like it better."

Sawyer started to say something else, but Sam Reed's attention had already been drawn elsewhere. He was a very busy man.

As the track was laid across Nebraska, it was followed by several entrepreneurial businessmen who traded in things as diverse as personal toiletries, writing material, and, of course, its most profitable enterprise: whiskey. They established their businesses in tents that could be moved as the track progressed. Because of that, the little settlements were referred to as End of Track. However, the whiskey dens, bawdy houses, and lowlifes that the mobile community attracted made many call the settlements Hell on Wheels.

The saloon tent proudly took that name for itself. The bar in Hell on Wheels consisted of a plank stretched across two barrels. Emil Sawyer and several other buffalo hunters were getting drunker, and angrier, as they discussed the turn of events that took away their livelihood.

"Gents, we don't have to put up with it," Sawyer said when he figured he had enough of them drunk and angry enough to go along with his plan.

"Whaddaya mean we don't have to put up with it?" one of the others slurred.

"Whoever sold the railroad the cattle has the money with them. Money that, by rights, should be ours," Sawyer said.

"Yeah, it should be ours," another agreed.

"Then I say let's go get it."

"Go get it? Whaddaya mean?"

"I mean let's go take it away from them," Sawyer said. "It won't be that hard."

"How do you know it won't be hard? There's no tellin' how many men there are in that outfit."

"There are only four men, and five women," Sawyer said, reporting what he had learned from Coleman. He knew nothing about Ollie Turner having joined them. "And get this, boys. One of the women is a whore."

Drunken smiles spread across the faces of the others.

"Five women, you say?"

"That's right. So, what do you gents say?"

"I say, let's go get our money," one of the others said.

"And the women," another added, and they all laughed.

Sawyer laughed with them. He wanted his share of the money as much as anyone else did, but it wasn't just the money that was driving him. He wanted to get even for the dirty trick they had pulled on him back in Mudflats.

By the time the Hodson Outfit was ready to start back to Texas, the chuck wagon was pretty well worn out. They abandoned the wagon and loaded everything they would need to make the trip back on the backs of the two mules. Ron was leading one of the mules, while Priscilla led the other.

The Hodson Outfit was returning with just under eighty thousand dollars in cash.

There had been some discussion as to how they would divide up the losses they had sustained during the drive.

Dooley and Kitty came up with a formula in which they divided the loss by sixteen. The women each sustained one-sixteenth of the loss, while the men took one-eighth of the loss. They also agreed that Ollie and Opal should be paid for their work and the agreed-upon fee was divided in the same way.

Although Opal had thought she would never return to Texas, she was now doing so willingly. But she wasn't going back to the Panhandle. Instead, she was going to El Paso with Ollie.

"With the money you good folks have paid us, we plan to get married and buy a little piece of land there," Ollie explained. "And if there really are wild cows for the taking as you say, why, I reckon we can start us a ranch. You have a drive like this next year, and we'll bring our cows up to go with you. It'll be nice, pushin' our own cattle."

"We'd be glad to have you as partners next year," Dick said.

Despite the fact that they didn't get as much money as they thought they would, the money they did get would be enough to save their ranches, thus everyone was returning in good spirits. And if cattle prices didn't come up by next year, they would drive the cows to someplace where they could get a decent price.

"By next year the railroad will be all through Nebraska," Dick explained. "If we had to, we could drive them up to the rail-head, then ship them on to Chicago. I know some people in the Chicago stockyards. They'll pay a decent price, and be glad to get the cattle."

It was Anita who first became aware that several men were dogging them, riding par-allel, and for the most part staying out of sight. They were good, but Anita was better, and she was on to them almost as soon as they started shadowing the trail.

"We're being followed," she told Buck, who was riding alongside her.

"How many?"

"I've made out ten so far," Anita replied. "Eight back here, and two more riding ahead of the main bunch."

"Better tell Dick."

Anita moved up to where Dick and Marline were riding side by side. She came up alongside and reported what she had spotted.

"Don't give away that you've seen them," Dick said.

"If they're watchin' as close as I think they are, they for sure saw me come up to talk to you," Anita replied. "They'll have to figure it was about somethin'."

"Laugh," Marline suggested.

"What?"

"Laugh, like Dick just told you a joke. They wouldn't figure you to be laughing if you are reporting that you've spotted them."

"Yes, good idea," Anita said. She laughed, and Dick and Marline joined in the laughter.

"Don't be obvious about it, but tell the others," Dick said. "Tell them to be ready to move on my signal."

"Right," Anita said, slapping her legs against the side of her horse and sloping off down the hill toward the others.

Sawyer held up his hand and those who were riding with him stopped.

"They'll be comin' through this pass any time now," he said, pointing to a notch between two hills. "And when they do, we'll shoot 'em down like dogs."

"The women, too?" one of the men asked.

"The women, too."

"I don't know, Sawyer," the man said, rubbing himself. "It sure would be nice to have me a woman 'bout now."

"Jake, you dumb bastard, don't you know there ain't a woman down there who wouldn't rather die than go with you?"

Jake leaned over to spit out a stream of tobacco, leaving a drizzle of it on his chin. "Yeah, I reckon you're right," he said.

"Then, if you think of it that way, we'll be doin' them a favor," Sawyer said. "Now, get ready."

"I'm ready," Jake said.

Sawyer looked at the nine men he had with him. He had known four of them during the war, because they had ridden with the same Jayhawker outfit he had ridden with. Ironically, two of the others had ridden with Quantrill. They had been bitter enemies then, but they were now allied in the same dastardly cause.

Sawyer looked at the little opening where Hodson and his people would soon appear. All of his men were well armed, well mounted, concealed, and had the advantage of surprise. They'd shoot Hodson and the others down before the cowpokes knew what hit them.

Sawyer cocked his pistol and stared straight ahead.

And he waited.

"Sawyer, where the hell are they?" Jake

called. "Shouldn't they be comin' through by now?"

Sawyer stood in his stirrups and looked down toward the pass in confusion. He scratched his head.

"Hey, mister, you lookin' for us?" Dick called down to him.

As soon as they got behind a hill, Dick had signaled to the others to follow him. Then, riding hard and staying in defilade, they had rounded the hill to come up behind anyone who might be watching them.

"The sons of bitches are behind us!" Sawyer shouted, then raised his rifle and fired.

Buck's horse reared then fell, and Buck had to roll to one side to avoid being crushed. He leaped to his feet and tried to catch the horse, but it darted away, leaving Buck afoot, his pistol in his hand.

One of the buffalo hunters galloped toward him, smiling broadly at the prospect of an easy kill. Buck fired, and the buffer pitched out of his saddle. There was no cover and Buck was out in the open and unmounted — not a good place to be. Another horseman loomed on his right, and Buck fired again. His bullet hit the horse and it stumbled, throwing the rider over his head.

Ron galloped up to him then and yanked

Buck up onto his own horse behind him. The two men galloped to the cover of a nearby group of boulders. Buck slid down from the horse and ran to one of the rocks as a bullet whistled by his ear. He squeezed off another shot and saw a hat fly.

Anita, Priscilla, and Kitty came to join him then, their own guns roaring, smoke billowing out before them.

Sawyer suddenly realized that most of his men were now gone, either lying dead in the dirt or riding off somewhere, carrying lead and bleeding from their wounds. Enraged at the way things had turned out, he stood and yelled toward the rocks where, by now, Dick Hodson and his entire group had taken shelter.

"Hodson!" Sawyer yelled, remembering the name Coleman had told him. "Dick Hodson!"

"I'm here," Dick called back to him.

"Let's have it out, boy. Me an' you!" Sawyer put his pistol in his holster and held his arms out by his sides.

Dick slipped his own pistol into his holster, but before he could step out, Buck put his hand on Dick's arm.

"Why don't you let me do that?" he said. "I'm faster than you, and it wouldn't do now for us to lose you."

Dick looked at Buck and saw the sincerity in the young man's face. He put his hand on Buck's shoulder.

"You may be faster, boy, but I've killed a hell of a lot more," he said. He stepped out from behind the rock and faced Sawyer.

Sawyer glared at Hodson for a long moment, his eyes glowering with hate. Blood was running down his forehead from a nick on the top of his head.

"You been a thorn in my side, boy," he said. "First there was that little stunt you pulled on me an' my friends down in Mudflats. Then you put me out of work by selling your damn cows to the railroad. I'm going to enjoy killing you."

"How do you plan to do that, mister? By talking me to death?"

With a yell of defiance, Sawyer went for his pistol. Buck might have been right — he may have been faster than Dick — but on this occasion, Dick was certainly fast enough. He had his pistol out in the blink of an eye. Despite that, Sawyer still managed to get off the first shot, though as it was hurried, the bullet whizzed by. Dick returned fire, and his bullet hit Sawyer in the chest, knocking him backward. Dick held the smoking gun in his hand, ready to fire again, but Sawyer lay dead with a single bullet in his heart. Dick holstered his pistol.

The impromptu battlefield was silent now, and Dick and the others stood up cautiously to look out over what they had done. Besides Sawyer, five of the men who had been with him were dead. Four others had ridden off to lick their wounds.

"Let's go home," Dick said.

CHAPTER NINETEEN

Windom, Texas

The first thing Bryan Phelps did after buying out Reba Driscoll was to clear away the charred remains of the barn. Then he had the main house and all the outbuildings razed so he could build a house befitting the cattle empire he was putting together from all the ranches he had taken over.

Even though Phelps was a bachelor and had no need of such grandeur, he was insistent that the house be the largest in the Texas Panhandle. He called the mansion American Eagle, and it awed everyone who saw it, for it was gigantic, with cupolas and dormers and so many windows that the sun flashed back with such brilliance that it almost looked as if the house were on fire.

The house reminded many of a wedding cake, white and tiered. A large, white-graveled driveway made a "U" through the beautifully landscaped lawn in front of the house.

Priscilla saw the house when she returned triumphantly from the long trail drive. She arrived home at about eleven o'clock one night, anxiously anticipating the moment she would crest Crowley Ridge and see her house. But the huge, white edifice that gleamed in the moonlight was obviously out of place here.

Ron Sietz found her a short while later, sitting on top of the hill, just staring down at the strange house where her own should have been. He took her in his arms.

"Your mom and your brothers are safe," he said. "They're in Fort Worth."

"And my pa?"

"I'm sorry," Ron said, pulling her more tightly to him. "You'll be staying with us," he said.

Trudy Konda had held onto the Tilting K in the desperate hope that Marline would return with enough money to save it. Indeed, Marline brought back enough to ensure that the taxes would be paid the next year, but the victory was bittersweet, considering that her father was not here to share it with them.

"But with McCamey Creek dammed up

we won't have enough water," Trudy said. "So I think we need to seriously decide whether or not we want to save the ranch."

"You'll keep the ranch," Dick said. "And McCamey Creek."

"How?"

"I have an idea," Dick said. "But it's going to take me a few days to put it into effect."

There was a party on the front lawn of American Eagle. Tables were set up on the neatly clipped turf, and they were all covered with white linen and spread with an array of food, drinks, china, and fine crystal. Well-dressed men and women were standing around in groups as servants flitted about, carrying trays of drinks. A chamber orchestra was playing on the porch.

Some of the partygoers had lived in the Panhandle for a long time. Most of the guests, though, were like Bryan Phelps. They had moved down after the war to take advantage of the opportunities turmoil and hard times had created for the enterprising person.

There was no end to Phelps' conniving, for the purpose of this party was to form a committee to petition the United States to break the Panhandle away from the rest of

Texas, annex the Cimarron Strip, and create a new state to be called Cimarron. Naturally, Phelps intended to be the governor.

Those who knew of Phelps' plan had already eagerly endorsed it, hoping for some reward for their early support. Because they were busy making plans for the future of Cimarron, only a handful of them noticed the approach of a rider who was driving about half a dozen cows before him. Those who noticed him paid little attention to him, as they assumed he was merely one of the ranch hands. Most looked away to redirect their attention to the conversation at hand, or to enjoy the music, food, and drink of the party.

But suddenly there was a crashing sound, the bawl of a confused steer, and the scream of a frightened woman. Everyone looked back around then, and they realized with shock that the cowboy was driving the cattle right through the lawn party! Tables were knocked over and chairs were brushed aside as the party guests scattered to avoid the animals. A huge silver punch bowl, the centerpiece of the largest table, was turned over, spilling its dark, red liquid upon the lap of one of the women guests.

Phelps stood there in confused shock.

Then he recognized the cowboy, and he shouted in anger.

"Hodson! Hodson, what the hell do you think you are doing?"

Dick stopped his horse and hooked one leg across the pommel of his saddle, then sat there, looking down at Phelps.

"Why, I just wanted to get your attention, Colonel," he said. "That is what you call yourself isn't it? Colonel?"

Phelps fought hard to show restraint. He wanted everyone present to see how he would handle himself as their governor. He forced a laugh. "Well, young man, you certain managed to do that," he said.

Several of his guests laughed nervously.

"Now that you have my attention, what do you want?"

"The dam on McCamey Creek. I want you to take it down."

"I can't do that," Phelps said. "That dam is needed to provide an efficient water supply for my ranch."

"You bring it down today, or I'll bring it down tomorrow morning," Dick said.

"How do you plan to do that?"

"By any means necessary," Dick said, jerking his horse around, then urging it into a quick trot.

As Dick rode away, Phelps called

Coleman over to him. "Get some men together," he said quietly. "And get them out to that dam."

"Colonel, you aren't going to take the dam down, are you?" Coleman asked, surprised by the request.

"No, you idiot," Phelps snarled. "Hodson has been a thorn in my side ever since you failed to stop him on the trail. When he comes out there tomorrow, I intend to have enough men to take care of him once and for all."

When Dick returned to Trailback, he saw Ollie working on a piece of weaponry. There were several others standing around him, watching him as he worked.

"I see you got it," Dick said, smiling as he swung down from his saddle. "Did you have any trouble?"

"Not a bit. And it only cost us one hundred dollars. I paid off one of the guards at the armory."

"Will it do the job?"

Ollie ran his hand along the bronze barrel. "A twelve-pounder Napoleon?" he said. "You better believe it. As far as I'm concerned, it was the finest piece of ordnance in our entire inventory. Trust me, if you want that dam brought down, this baby will do it."

"How much ammunition did you get?"

"There are ten balls and twenty-five pounds of powder in the ammunition chest. That's more than enough."

Dooley laughed. "I'm going to enjoy seeing the expression on Phelps' face in the morning when he sees what we've got in store for him."

McCamey Creek Dam

Behind Dick, the horizon showed a thin line of gray. In half an hour it would be light enough to see. Dick had told Phelps that if the dam didn't come down during the day, that he would take it down the next morning . . . this morning. Implied in that statement was the fact that Dick wouldn't even show up until morning when, in fact, he and his entire outfit had come out in the middle of the night.

Last night, when the moon was at its brightest, Ollie had laid the gun in, in preparation of using it today. He already had the powder separated into charges, and he had a little pile of twelve-pound solid shot ready to go.

During the night they had heard the sounds of several horses and men, so he knew that Phelps was doing exactly what he thought he would do — he was setting up an ambush. Now, by the gray light of early morning, he could see that Phelps, Coleman, and at least ten more men were in position in the rocks on each side of the creek, and on the dam. They moved quickly into position and would have been ideally situated to spring an ambush when Dick arrived, if Dick and the others approached from the Tilting K.

But Dick and the others were already there, in place and ready to commence the operation when the time was right. Marline stood right beside Dick. Looking to his left, he saw that Ollie and Opal were in position around the cannon. Then he saw Buck and Anita, Dooley and Kitty, and Ron and Priscilla, also ready. It wasn't that they were unaware of the danger facing them this morning — indeed, they were keenly aware. They just wanted to face the danger together.

"Coleman, you get over there," Phelps' voice carried back to Dick. "When they show up, wait until I give the word. Then start blasting away. I want Hodson and everyone with him killed."

"He might have them women with him," someone said.

"I don't care who he has with him, I want them all killed!" Phelps shouted.

Phelps was standing by the edge of the creek, looking up the road toward the Tilting K, from where he believed Dick and the others would come. Dick quietly jacked a round into the chamber of his rifle, then drew a bead on Phelps' chest. He could drop him from this distance, and Phelps would never know what hit him. It wasn't a very sporting way to kill a man.

Dick held that position for a long moment, not quite ready to kill a man from ambush. Then he remembered Antietam, and the job his commander had given him to do. As the best rifle marksman in the company, Dick had been given the job of sniper. He lost track of the number of men he killed in that battle, and none of the men he killed ever saw the man who pulled the trigger. They had been good men, soldiers who were fighting for what they believed in. It just so happened they were wearing a different uniform. If he could kill *decent* men in such a way, he should have no compunctions about squeezing the trigger on this low-down buzzard.

"Go to hell, Phelps," Dick said under his breath.

The rifle barked and kicked back against

his shoulder. He saw a puff of dust rise from Phelps' chest, saw the carpetbagger raise his hands in surprise, then fall down.

Dick's shot was the signal for Ollie and, even as the men down at the dam were wondering what had happened to their leader, the thunderous roar of the Napoleon twelve-pounder shook the ground. The cannon was well laid in, and the first shot hit right in the middle of the dam. There was no explosive charge in the shell, but its weight was such that the dam blew apart just as if it had been mined with blasting powder. Dick saw, also, that three of Phelps' men had gone down with that first round.

Now the others in Dick's group began firing as well. Dick saw one of Phelps' men get up and try to run, only to be cut down. Pistol- and riflefire rippled back and forth, then returned as echoes as the two groups fired at each other. He heard screams of pain, curses of fury, and he saw men crumple, grabbing their guts, or falling back dead before they hit the ground.

By now, Ollie and Priscilla had reloaded the Napoleon, and it roared a second time. This shot completed what the first had started, and the dam, now completely destroyed, gave way as the water behind it began rushing through.

"Hold it! Hold on!" Coleman started shouting when the roar of the last cannon blast rolled away. Dick saw a white handkerchief being waved down by where the dam had been just a few moments earlier.

"Cease fire!" Dick shouted, and the shooting stopped.

"Don't shoot no more!" Coleman said. Cautiously, he came out into the open, holding his hands up over his head.

"Call the others out as well," Dick said.

Coleman looked around for a moment, then he looked back toward Dick. "What others?" he called. "I'm the only one left."

Dick came out from behind the rock and started walking toward Coleman. "I ought to kill you where you stand," he said, cocking the rifle.

"No, please!" Coleman said, holding his hands out in front of him, as if by that action he could ward off any bullets.

"You got a horse?" Dick asked.

"Yeah, I got a horse."

"Get on him and git," Dick said. "Don't ever come back, Coleman. Never. If I ever see you again, I'll kill you on sight. Do you understand that?"

"Y-yes sir, I understand," Coleman said contritely.

Even as he was speaking, Anita Votaw

was bringing a horse to him.

"That . . . that ain't my horse," Coleman said, nervously.

"It's the one you're ridin' out of here," Dick said. "Get on him."

Coleman climbed onto the horse, then took the reins. "You got no right to . . ." he started, but before he could finish, Buck slapped the side of the horse.

"Heeaaayyhh!" Buck shouted. The horse bolted forward, and Coleman jerked in his saddle, barely able to hang on.

By now, Ollie and Opal had left the cannon and stood there with Dick and Marline, Ron and Priscilla, Buck and Anita, and Dooley and Kitty. All were still holding the guns that had carried out their work with deadly efficiency. The morning air was perfumed with the smell of cordite, but the roar of gunfire had been replaced by the rush of water as McCamey Creek filled and began flowing toward the Tilting K. When he was sure that there was no more danger, Dick put away his gun, and the others followed suit.

"Folks, me'n Opal got somethin' to ask you," Ollie said. "I mean, she's got no folks, and truth to tell, I don't know whether I got anyone left down in El Paso or not. So, well, we was just wonderin' if maybe you'd all stand up for us at our wedding."

"No," Dick said.

The others looked at Dick in surprise.

"What?" Marline asked, shocked by Dick's reply.

Dick smiled broadly. "We'll do a lot more than stand up for you," he said. "We'll throw the entire wedding for you. You'll get married at Trailback, and it'll be the biggest wedding Hutchinson County has seen since the war."

"Now that's more like it," Marline said.

"You don't have to go to all that trouble," Ollie said. "Just get a preacher to say a few words, is all."

"Sure I do," Dick replied. He put his arm around Marline, then looked at the other couples. "It'll be good practice. The way I got it figured, there's going to be quite a few of 'em in the next few weeks."

"Damn," Priscilla said.

"What?" Anita asked, surprised by Priscilla's outburst.

"Here, the four of us made that star pattern quilt, sayin' it would go to the first one of us to get married and who's goin' to get it but Opal?"

"Great," Marline said, smiling at Opal. "I can't think of a more decent person to receive it."